PATTI JO MOORE

An Unexpected Romance

Patti Jo Moore

ISBN-13: 978-1-0880-3526-9

Dedicated to my precious family and friends who continue to encourage me. Very special thanks to Hugh, Dr. Amy, Becca, Steven, Shaun, John, Eleanor, Janet, and Nancy. Also Kathy, Norma, Vickie, Susan & Jim, Pam, Lisa, Celia, Debbie B., Veronica B., Carlotta, and Debbie M. A special shout-out to Sandra Orchard, Debby Giusti, Helen Gray, Tina Radcliffe, my Writing Sisters, and Mallory Bordelon Williams. With appreciation also to Cynthia Hickey and Sherri Stewart. I am so thankful for my Lord Jesus Christ, who blesses me in unexpected ways. May my words always honor Him.

Chapter 1

Gracie Norton opened her front door and froze. Was someone crying? How strange. The unmistakable whimpers of a young child became more obvious as she stepped onto the small front porch to water her thirsty ferns. Even though she had only lived in this Florida neighborhood for a month, she'd never noticed any young children living close by. Maybe one of her neighbors had visitors. She poured water into two of her hanging baskets, then returned to her kitchen sink to refill her watering can.

When Gracie finished watering her plants she noticed a pick-up truck parked in the driveway next door. Hmm...maybe someone had bought the house. She hadn't seen the realtor's sign since the week before. Hidden behind a large fern, she peeked around to see a tall, broad-shouldered man carrying a box into the house. Could he be her new neighbor?

Feeling foolish for snooping like a busybody, Gracie was heading into the house when her cell phone rang.

She answered to hear her best friend, Kira, giggling. "You sound out of breath. Were you exercising?"

No way would she tell Kira she'd been snooping on the new neighbor. Her engaged friend had tried to convince Gracie to start dating again, but she wasn't ready. "No, I wasn't exercising, although that's a good idea with all the baking I enjoy. Are we still on for this evening?"

"You bet! How about if I pick you up around six o'clock? Is the Happy Fisherman Restaurant still okay with you?"

"Yes, I can't wait. I've been so hungry for a good seafood meal. I'll be ready at six."

She needed to shower, but first she'd make sure her back door was locked. As she checked the doorknob, something in the small backyard caught her eye and she did a double-take. A yellow ball. Where did that come from?

Unlocking the door, she hurried out to take a closer look. A voice from her left surprised her, and a sweet little face peered at her through the chain-link fence.

"I'm sorry our ball wented in your yard." The young girl appeared to be four or five years old, and she gazed at Gracie with innocent, brown eyes.

"It's okay, sweetie. Here you go." Gracie carefully tossed the ball over the fence but was startled when an adult voice called to the child.

"Trixie, you need to come inside now." The

man she'd seen minutes earlier walked toward the fence, pausing about five feet away. His dark eyes held a hint of curiosity, but he didn't smile.

Gracie approached the fence, offering a gracious smile as she spoke. "Are you my new neighbor? I'm Gracie Norton, and I'd noticed your child's ball over here so I came out to return it."

He nodded and the hint of a smile appeared on his handsome face. "Yes, I'm Blake Donovan and this is my daughter, Trixie. Her twin brother, Max, is in the house. We've just moved in today. I'm sorry about the ball." He shoved his hands into his jeans pockets, as if uncomfortable talking with a stranger.

Gracie offered a reassuring smile to the child. "It's no problem if a ball lands in my yard." She remembered the whimpering she'd heard earlier and hoped he hadn't scolded the child about the ball going over the fence. "It's nice meeting you both, and I look forward to meeting Max. I hope you'll be happy living in Coastal Breeze. I've only lived here a month but already love it. Not to mention being on the Florida panhandle and so close to the beach." She winked at Trixie, who'd been watching her with interest.

Blake nodded. "Thanks. We moved from Gainesville, Florida, so the kids are excited to be closer to the coast now."

As much as she'd like to find out more about her new neighbors, Gracie needed to shower and get ready to go out with her friend. "It was nice meeting you, and I hope you'll have a good evening." She didn't miss the shadow that passed over Trixie's face—as if not wanting to say good-bye.

Minutes later as water ran over her, thoughts of her new neighbors ran through her mind. Blake Donovan hadn't mentioned a wife, so Gracie assumed he must be a single dad. How sad, because his twins were still so young.

There was one thing she was sure of—Trixie was adorable and the dad was quite handsome. She had no complaints about neighbors like that—no complaints at all.

~ ~ ~

"Daddy and me got to meet the lady next door!" Trixie announced to her twin brother as she burst into the house in excitement.

Five-year-old Max glanced up from putting away toy blocks, obviously more interested in seeing the yellow ball. "Oh, you got the ball back." A smile vanished as he gazed up sheepishly at his father. "I won't throw the ball near the fence again, Dad."

"Good boy." Blake ruffled his son's dark brown hair, touched by his sincere statement. "Now let's finish putting things away. Max, you've done a good job picking up those scattered blocks, so now I need you and Trixie to carry these small boxes to your new bedrooms. After we get more things unpacked, we'll go pick up supper, okay?" He'd already decided to treat the twins to a hamburger meal complete with milkshakes. Just a little something to give them a lift, because he knew this move hadn't been easy on them, either. Now seeing their heads bob eagerly at the mention of picking up supper, he made a mental note to do more special activities with his children. Especially now that his work schedule had improved.

As he hung his clothes in the master bedroom closet, Blake's mind drifted back to the neighbor he and Trixie met minutes earlier. *Gracie Norton.* Tall, slender, with gorgeous auburn hair hanging on her shoulders. Even though she'd smiled and spoken in a friendly tone, there had been something guarded in her green eyes. Or maybe that was only his imagination.

Blake's ringing cell phone snapped him from his thoughts of the beautiful neighbor. Seeing his buddy, Sarge's name on the caller ID, Blake couldn't suppress a grin. "Hey, Sarge."

"Howdy, Blake. Just wanted to check on you and the kids. Nora said she sure wished you all lived close by, because she's cooked a pot of soup and would love to share."

A tug at his heart caused Blake to hesitate before replying. The truth was he also wished they lived closer to Sarge and Nora. The middle-aged couple had been godsends for him and the twins when Blake's wife had lost her battle with cancer two years earlier. "Please tell Nora that I'm sure her soup is delicious. And I promise we'll head over that way for a visit before long. The twins miss their Aunt Nora and Uncle Sarge."

The two men talked a few more minutes before the call ended. As Blake put clothes and shoes in his closet, he thought about his friend. The age difference between the two men didn't matter, because they shared a friendship that had grown stronger over time.

When Blake first began his job as a pharmaceutical representative, Sarge had taken the younger man under his wing and helped him. Assuming that Sarge had been in the military, Blake later learned that his real name was Greg, but his wife had teasingly bestowed the nickname on him because she thought he often acted like a drill sergeant.

"We finished our work, Dad." A rumpled-haired Max appeared at Blake's bedroom door, his shirt bearing the jelly stain from his lunch.

"Good job, son. Let's get your hair combed and then you'll need a clean shirt. I'll make sure Trixie is wearing clean clothes too, and then we'll go pick up our supper."

"Can Pedro go with us?" Trixie asked hopefully.

Blake didn't want to disappoint her but knew the drive would go smoother without the beloved family dog. He shook his head and patted Trixie's shoulder. "Not this time. Pedro still needs to get used to his new home here, and we won't be gone long." He was relieved when his daughter nodded and grabbed her favorite stuffed toy, a rabbit named Roscoe.

Fifteen minutes later Blake and the twins were headed to a fast-food burger place on the outskirts of Coastal Breeze. As the children chattered happily in the back seat, Blake smiled at their playful comments. Poor little kids—they'd only been two and a half when their mother had died, so their memories of her were limited. Until recently, Blake's job required frequent travel, which had been another hardship. He was thankful that he'd convinced his district boss to cut back on his traveling.

Heading back with their meals, Blake cautioned the children to be careful with the milkshakes. "Remember, you can finish the shakes after your supper. I don't want you filling up on them, even though I know they're good." He grinned while glancing in his rearview mirror.

When he pulled into the driveway, Trixie exclaimed. "Look, there's our new neighbor! She's nice."

Blake turned in time to see Gracie and another woman heading into her house. Hmm…if she was with a female friend, did that mean she was single? *Get a grip, Donovan. Just because she's been out with a friend doesn't mean she's single. Married women have friends too.*

He forced his thoughts away from his neighbor and focused on his children. Helping them out of the car and making sure the milkshakes remained intact required his attention. He didn't have time to think about the attractive woman next door.

Besides, Blake had no room in his life for a romantic interest at the present time. He had young children to care for and a job that still required some travel. So that left no time to pursue romance.

But it sure wouldn't hurt to be a friendly neighbor to Gracie Norton. And it wouldn't hurt his eyes, either.

~ ~ ~

The next morning Gracie hurried out her door so she wouldn't be late to church. A September breeze blew in from the gulf, sending strands of her auburn hair into her face. She smoothed it away and climbed into her car, replaying comments from the previous night in her mind.

When Gracie and Kira had returned from their seafood meal, the new neighbor pulled into his driveway at the same time and Kira caught a glimpse of him. Later as the two women sat at Gracie's kitchen table sipping coffee and visiting, her friend made more than a few comments about the handsome man next door. It didn't matter that Gracie knew very little about him because Kira was determined to keep mentioning him.

Now as she hurried into the worship building, Gracie hoped Kira wouldn't mention her neighbor again. Spotting her friend seated on the right side, Gracie slipped onto the pew beside her. "Whew, glad I made it before the music started." As if on cue, the pianist began the prelude and the choir entered.

The worship service passed quickly with a meaningful sermon and uplifting music. Gracie was thankful to have such a wonderful church so close to home, and she was also thankful Kira made the drive from Destin to attend with her.

After the service ended, the two friends headed toward the door, greeted by many church members before leaving. Although still somewhat a newcomer, Gracie knew she truly belonged in this small community.

To her relief, Kira didn't mention the handsome new neighbor, instead asking about her plans for the day. "Is it your weekend to check on the boarded pets at the animal clinic?"

Gracie shook her head while pulling her keys from her handbag. "No, one of the other assistants has that duty. Since it looks like we'll get some rain, I'm glad to have an afternoon at home with my cats and a novel I want to read." She giggled and rolled her eyes. "Good grief, I sound like a spinster, don't I?"

Kira patted her arm. "No, actually your afternoon sounds relaxing. I'm heading to my parents' house to help my mom clean out a closet." The wind picked up and thunder rumbled in the distance, so the friends hugged good-bye and hurried to their cars.

As she drove the short distance to her home, Gracie thought about Kira's afternoon plans. She knew her friend was thankful to have her parents nearby even if they demanded quite a bit of Kira's time.

The rain had started and fat drops splattered on the windshield as Gracie pulled into her driveway. Releasing a sigh, she wondered for the thousandth time how things would be if her own parents were still alive. *No, I refuse to be in a melancholy mood today.* The silent chiding was something she'd repeated to herself numerous times in the past three years.

That afternoon as she ate a bowl of soup and began a new romance novel, Gracie glanced up to see her orange cat returning her gaze. She released a sigh as she commented aloud to the feline. "Yes, it's ironic, isn't it, Cheddar? I'm through with romance in my life—at least for a long time—but yet I still enjoy reading these Christian romance novels." She shook her head at herself as Cheddar curled up in his cat bed.

About mid-afternoon Gracie heard a car door close. Who was that? She wasn't expecting anyone today. Peering out her living room window, she saw a car parked in Blake's driveway. A tall, brunette woman strode to her neighbor's door. After the woman disappeared from Gracie's line of vision, curiosity ran through her, which was silly. Why should she care if the single dad had a girlfriend?

But thoughts of precious Trixie and her twin brother flashed through her mind, and she knew the real reason she cared about Blake's dating life. Those children were still young, so Gracie hoped whoever their father dated would be good to the twins, especially if their mother was deceased. It had been difficult enough when she'd lost her parents in her twenties, but the thought of such young children losing their mother pierced her heart. She determined right then that whenever the opportunity arose, she'd pay extra attention to the twins next door because the expression on Trixie's face still tugged at her thoughts.

~ ~ ~

"Daddy, Aunt Brianna is here!" Trixie's voice reached Blake's ears as he placed items in an overnight bag.

Stepping into the living room, Blake grinned at his younger sister. "Sorry you had to drive in the rain. Was the traffic bad?"

The twenty-two-year-old shook her head. "Nah, it just took a little longer thanks to the weather, but you know I don't mind driving. And I'm just coming from Pensacola, so it's not like I live in Miami." She grinned at her niece and nephew, then patted Max on the head. "Besides, knowing I was headed to see my two favorite kiddos in the whole world is worth any drive."

Blake had already told his children he was leaving on a short business trip, but they'd have fun with their aunt. Now Trixie peered up at him with a shadow of apprehension on her small face. "When will you be back, Daddy?"

Her question sent a stab of guilt to his heart, and he leaned down to embrace her in a warm hug. Even though his children knew their father had to travel with his job now and then, they didn't want him to be away very long. Thanks to his understanding manager, Blake's traveling time had been greatly reduced. Still, he longed for a job that didn't take him away from his children at all.

"I'll be back tomorrow by supper time, sweetie. And then I shouldn't have to travel any more for a while."

Brianna leaned down to Trixie's eye level. "Hey, kiddo. We've got some games to play, so you won't even know your dad isn't here. Let's see...which should we play first? Candy Land or hide-and-seek?" She pretended to be deep in thought. It worked like a charm because the twins both squealed in delight, bouncing up and down.

Blake smiled at his sibling and leaned toward her. "Thanks, sis. I owe you big time." He wasn't sure what he would've done without her. Even before he and the children moved much closer to Brianna, she'd driven over to central Florida at various times to help out with the twins. But now they were all in the Florida panhandle, so at least she didn't have to drive such a distance.

At her brother's compliment, Brianna shook her head. "Hey, you've given me a wonderful niece and nephew, so I think we're even." She tweaked Trixie's nose before adding another comment directed at Blake. "Besides, I'm just thankful you were able to schedule this trip so I wouldn't have to miss any classes."

He shook his head. "I'd never want you to miss your classes. The twins should be starting their new preschool next week, so that will help with childcare arrangements—at least a good bit of the time."

After making sure he had all the necessary paperwork for his meeting, Blake hugged the twins, thanked his sister again, and headed to his car. The familiar pulling at his heart seemed heavier than ever. How long could he continue doing this? He consoled himself with the fact that his twins adored their aunt, and the feeling was mutual. Yet his children still needed *him.* It was bad enough they'd lost their mother, but they didn't need a father who traveled. Something had to give.

At one point in his life, he might've prayed about the situation, but now he wasn't sure if God would listen to his prayers. After losing Lorie he'd pulled away from his Christian faith, feeling overwhelmed and devastated to be widowed with two young children. For six months after Lorie's passing, Blake kept questioning how a loving God could take a mother from her toddlers. His sadness had grown into anger, which led to drinking at times. Thanks to heart-to-heart talks with Sarge, the drinking had stopped. But he kept his distance from God. Blake figured he and the children would get by somehow.

Yet something was missing—besides a mother for his children and a wife for him. Maybe living in a new place would be good for all of them. Not to mention Coastal Breeze was much smaller than Gainesville, and now they were located on the coast. Surely, this feeling of discontent would vanish after they were settled and he and the children could take walks along the beach. With a long sigh, he told himself things would look brighter soon. If only he believed it.

~ ~ ~

When Blake arrived home the next afternoon, something was wrong. The look his sister gave him alerted him, and his pulse kicked up a notch. "How is everything?" He wasn't sure he wanted to hear her answer.

Brianna spoke softly. "The twins are fine. It's Pedro. He hasn't played like he normally does and he hasn't been eating. Just lying around. I didn't want to alarm the kiddos, so I told them that Pedro needs to rest. But I think they can tell he's not himself." Brianna shook her head, then continued. "I know you've just moved here, but you need to find a good animal clinic. I'll search online. Surely, there's one not too far away." She hurried to the kitchen table where her laptop was opened.

Before Blake could join her, the twins appeared in the living room. Two worried little faces peered up at him. Attempting to sound upbeat, Blake grinned at them. "Hey there, what have you two been doing? I was about to come and find you."

Trixie spoke up as usual. "We were doing puzzles in Max's room."

Max spoke hesitantly. "We're worried about Pedro." Blake could tell he was fighting tears.

Leaning down to their eye level, Blake took

their hands in his and spoke gently. "Pedro isn't feeling well, but he might just need some vitamins. You know how sometimes you don't feel very good, and you have to rest and take medicine?"

Both heads nodded slowly.

"Okay, well, animals get that way too. So Aunt Brianna is finding an animal doctor who can check Pedro, and hopefully he should be fine." *Yes, please let him be fine. My children don't need another loss in their lives.* He didn't think God would pay attention to a plea from him, but it made him feel better to offer the request on behalf of his children.

"Here we go." Brianna gestured to her laptop screen. Angling it so Blake could see the ad, Brianna read the name aloud. "Meows and Mutts Animal Clinic, and this ad says they've been in business for fifteen years, so they must be good."

Blake nodded, then glanced at his watch. "It's already after five o'clock, so I guess it's too late to get an appointment today. Hopefully they can see him tomorrow. I know you need to get on the road, Bri. Thanks so much for staying with the twins."

"We had fun, didn't we kiddos?" She ruffled Max's hair and grinned at the children, who both embraced her in a hug. With an apologetic look at her brother, she added. "If I didn't have class tomorrow morning I'd stay another night."

Blake shook his head. "You've already been a big help. Just be safe on your drive to

Pensacola. And I'll let you know what we find out about Pedro."

After his sister left, Blake fed the twins supper, thankful Brianna had prepared chili earlier that day and there was plenty left to reheat. He kept the children occupied with books that evening so they didn't continue asking questions about Pedro.

But before going to sleep later that night, Blake kept thinking about Pedro. He knew he'd do whatever was needed for the family pet because there was no way he'd let his children experience another loss in their young lives—not if he could help it.

~ ~ ~

Tuesday morning Gracie poured a cup of coffee and sat at a small table in the breakroom of Meows and Mutts Animal Clinic. Glancing over the day's schedule, she breathed a sigh of relief. Unless emergencies arose today shouldn't be too hectic. She liked staying busy, but some days were exhausting—both physically and emotionally. It was always difficult to see an animal suffering or one who wouldn't get better.

The canine for the eleven o'clock slot was a new patient. Hopefully, the dog would be easy to manage, unlike a few she'd assisted with at her previous job. So far at Meows and Mutts, the majority of pets who'd been brought in had been docile. Of course, she'd only been here a month, but so far, so good. Most importantly, she genuinely loved her job working with the animals.

The morning passed quickly, and at eleven o'clock, Gracie grabbed a new patient packet and entered the small examination room to meet the owner and get vital signs on the dog. Opening the door, Gracie released a surprised gasp. The adult and two children huddled around a medium-sized black Labrador were her new neighbors. Right away she noticed the worried expressions they all wore.

"Good morning. Nice to see you again." She smiled at Trixie and Blake, then turned her attention to the little boy, who appeared to be the most worried of the three. "You must be Max."

The child barely nodded his head, and Gracie had the sneaking suspicion he was fighting tears. Poor little guy.

Leaning down to eye level, she softly spoke. "Max, I met your dad and sister the other day, so now I'm glad to meet you. I'm Miss Gracie, and I'm going to help with your dog today. What's your dog's name?" Gracie had to suppress a grin as Trixie eagerly responded.

"Pedro! And he's sick."

Gracie stood and smiled at Trixie. "Pedro is a very nice name."

She faced Blake with her pen and folder ready. "Can you give me some information about Pedro? His symptoms and if he's been sick or had surgery in the past?"

Blake slightly shrugged. "As you know we've just moved in this past weekend. He started acting unwell Sunday, after I'd left on a business trip. When I returned yesterday, my sister told me Pedro hadn't been eating or playing with the kids." He ran a hand over his face. "As for surgeries, none except the neutering. He's always seemed healthy, and we got him as a puppy."

Gracie finished making notes. "Okay, thank you. Dr. Tatum is our veterinarian and he'll be in shortly, but first I need to weigh Pedro, check his temperature, and listen to his heart." She didn't miss the look of fascination in both twins' faces as they watched her every move.

With Blake's help, Gracie positioned the dog on the scale long enough to obtain his accurate weight. As she lifted Pedro from the scale, Blake's hand brushed against hers as he reached out to help. Tensing, her face warmed to a blush. What was wrong with her? She needed to pretend he was a random client and not the handsome man who lived next door. *Oh, Dr. Tatum...please hurry.*

"Okay, now that I have Pedro's information, we'll see what Dr. Tatum has to say. He should be in shortly." She offered a quick smile after opening the door and almost plowed into her boss.

Dr. Tatum grinned at her. "Going somewhere, Gracie? You look like you're in a hurry." His eyes held a teasing glint.

Gracie shook her head. "No, sir. I didn't realize you were heading in here so soon." She turned around, feeling foolish.

"Hello, I'm Dr. Bernie Tatum, and you've met my assistant, Miss Gracie. Let's see about this new patient." The middle-aged veterinarian winked at the twins and shook Blake's hand before focusing his attention on the canine.

During the dog's examination, Gracie remained by Dr. Tatum's side, forcing herself to concentrate on the animal rather than the good-looking man and adorable twins standing within feet of her.

After a thorough checkup and a few questions to Blake, Dr. Tatum announced that Pedro would be fine. Nothing more than a bacterial infection that a week of antibiotics should take care of, along with some rest.

Gracie didn't miss the obvious relief on Blake's face and the gentle way he squeezed each child's shoulder, as if reassuring them their pet would be okay.

Blake shook hands again with Dr. Tatum and offered his thanks. Then Gracie escorted the family and their pet to the main counter.

As Blake paid the bill, Gracie reached into a small candy jar concealed behind the counter. Then she leaned down to the twins, who were hovering close to their father and dog.

"Since Pedro gets a doggy treat, here's a little treat for each of you. *If* it's okay with your father." She added the second comment, hoping she hadn't acted out of turn with her neighbor.

Blake finished paying the bill and grinned at his children. "How nice. What do you say?"

The twins spoke in unison. "Thank you." The delight on their faces as they eyed the cherry lollipops melted Gracie's heart. They didn't unwrap them at first but cast questioning glances at Blake.

He nodded. "Yes, you may unwrap them, but don't let them touch anything." He offered a polite nod to Gracie and the receptionist.

Before heading out the door, Trixie waved with her free hand. "Bye, Miss Gracie. See you soon."

After the door closed, the receptionist was eyeing her. "Did that little girl tell you she'd see you soon?" Dora's eyebrows arched in curiosity.

Attempting a nonchalant tone, Gracie nodded. "Yes, they've recently moved into the house next door to me. Those twins are adorable." She reached for the next patient's folder.

Dora nodded in agreement. "Yes, they are. And their father is too."

Gracie hurried to the examination area to tidy the room in preparation for the next client. But she couldn't deny her coworker's statement. Blake Donovan was one handsome man.

~ ~ ~

Chapter 2

"See? Pedro is going to be just fine. But he needs to rest and get better, so let's not play fetch with him for a while, okay?" Blake was relieved when the twins nodded, and he was also relieved the doctor had given Pedro an encouraging diagnosis. It could've been much worse.

While the children ate sandwiches, Blake sent a quick text message about Pedro's medical appointment to Brianna. He knew she'd been worried about the family pet too.

Minutes later he sat at the table eating a ham sandwich, but almost choked when Trixie surprised him with a question. "Daddy, do you like Miss Gracie? I think she's pretty."

"She seems nice and she was nice to Pedro." Would his daughter realize he'd evaded her actual question? To his relief the twins began conversing about the games they'd play with Pedro after the dog was well.

Later that afternoon Blake's thoughts returned to his daughter's question about their neighbor. Even though he didn't want to admit it to his young child, he also found Gracie pretty. Which made it surprising that she was single. But why should he care about his neighbor's personal life? He had no time for romance. The only two women he'd gone out with since being widowed weren't his type at all. Both were arranged dates by well-meaning friends, but neither woman had been right for him. More importantly, neither of them struck him as caring much about children, and his twins were his top priority. Period.

So Blake had determined to be the best father he could be and to do the best job he could for his company. Yet a restlessness simmered under the surface, which made him wonder if things would ever get better. Although he was thankful to have a job as a pharmaceutical representative, that wasn't where his heart was. The ringing cell phone jarred him from his thoughts, and he grabbed it up without checking the caller ID. Surprise washed over him as he heard his boss's voice.

"Blake, it's Ed Whitley here. How are you?"

Uh oh. Had he forgotten to turn in a report or make an important call? Clearing his throat, Blake answered in a professional tone. "Hello, Mr. Whitley. I'm well, thank you. How are you?"

"Doing well, thanks. I guess you've moved to your new town by now? I'm sure the Gainesville office misses you, but I know you'll continue doing expert work."

"Yes, my twins and I are getting settled in our

new home and so far, we like this smaller area. I'm planning to start the children in a local preschool next week, so that will help with my childcare situation. Since they share a September birthday, they won't begin kindergarten until next year."

"Sounds good, Blake. I know it hasn't been easy for you being a single dad." Mr. Whitley paused, as if being respectful for Blake's widowed status. Then in a more upbeat tone, he continued. "The main reason for my call today—besides checking on you and your twins—is to let you know about the employee teamwork strategy we're implementing."

Blake remained silent, unsure if this would be a good thing or something that would make his life more complicated.

"The managers met yesterday, and we all agree that the new employees could greatly benefit from being paired with more experienced representatives. So, you are to be paired with Chantelle Dawson, a twenty-five-year-old who is smart and eager to learn the ropes in our company."

Blake's mind whirled as his boss's words sunk in. Chantelle sounded like a female name. Was his boss pairing him up with a young woman?

"Blake? Does this sound agreeable to you? She would shadow you on some appointments, and of course, you'd need to meet for evaluations a few times. But I have a good feeling about this arrangement and think it will benefit everyone involved. The clients *and* our employees."

What could he say? Obviously, his boss expected him to receive this news with enthusiasm, but Blake was not going to lie. He chose his words carefully and maintained a polite, professional tone.

"I will do what is expected of me, Mr. Whitley." *Well that sounded lackluster, but it's the best I can do.*

His boss chuckled as if expecting him to say more. "We're still working out the details, but this new pairing-up process should begin within the next two weeks. Miss Dawson lives in the Orlando area, but she's agreed to stay with a friend temporarily in Destin while she trains with you."

Great. Just great. Blake rubbed his forehead as he felt a headache coming on. At that moment Max and Trixie ran through the kitchen and squeals erupted.

Mr. Whitley's volume increased, although his tone remained cordial. "Anyway, you'll receive the details soon. I'm sure you'll handle this arrangement very well. And I will say that by doing this, you're adding a feather in your cap." He laughed heartily, as if he'd made a joke.

Blake forced out a polite chuckle that sounded fake. What else could he do? He thanked his boss for calling, assured him he'd do his best, and the call ended. Now to check on his children and see what prompted the squealing.

When he stepped into Trixie's bedroom, he found her cradling her stuffed bunny. Max was in his room playing with his dinosaurs, making the usual roars.

Trixie peered up at Blake with fear in her eyes. "Daddy, Max said he was going to take Roscoe and hide him." She grasped the bunny tighter.

"No, he won't do that. Why did he say that?" Max must have heard his name and now stood at his sister's doorway, a sheepish look on his little face.

"Max?" Blake was curious what had started the teasing. His twins normally played well together or each did their own thing. It was rare for them to squabble.

"I was playing. And Trixie had one of my dinosaurs."

As Blake returned his eyes to his daughter, he saw a shadow of guilt. He didn't have to say a word, because Trixie peered up at her father and nodded.

"I only wanted to use a dinosaur so Roscoe could have a pet."

If Blake's head hadn't reached the throbbing point, this situation would've been humorous. And cute. But at the moment, he wanted his children to play nicely. And he wanted his head to stop hurting so he could absorb the news his boss had given him.

"Trixie, next time you need to ask Max if you can use one of his dinosaurs, okay?"

She nodded, holding Roscoe even closer to her chest.

"And Max, if there's a problem, you don't need to chase your sister through the house.

Especially when I'm on the phone. Okay?"

Max nodded, clearly eager to return to the small, plastic dinosaurs in his bedroom.

"Play with your toys while I take some medicine for my headache. Later we'll have a story together." Before Blake had taken three steps toward the kitchen for his medicine, he heard Max's voice.

"Here, Trixie. Roscoe can play with this one." Max had retrieved a toy dinosaur from his room and held it out to his sister.

The sight caused a lump to form in Blake's throat. Seeing Max share with Trixie reassured him that his children cared about each other, no matter how young they were.

Less than an hour later, his headache had eased, and Blake treasured special time with his twins as he read stories to them. If only he could forget about his boss's phone call and someone named Chantelle.

~ ~ ~

This couldn't be happening. Gracie glanced at her watch and sighed. *Why* wasn't her car starting? She had just enough time to arrive at the animal clinic and have her usual coffee before preparing for clients. She tried one more time and groaned. Might as well face it—her car was not starting. She only hoped whatever the problem was wouldn't involve large amounts of money.

For a few seconds, she sat in her car, unsure what to do. Then an idea formed that caused her heart rate to quicken, but what other choice did she have? She couldn't very well ask Dr. Tatum to leave the clinic and come to her aid.

Hesitation made her inch toward Blake's front door. What if his children were sleeping? She'd feel terrible if she woke them. Rapping at the door, Gracie practically held her breath. She was about to knock again, but her hand froze as the door swung open.

Blake's curious expression only increased her already rapid heartbeat. His dark hair was slightly mussed, as if he'd not combed it yet, and he wore jeans and a t-shirt. Even in a casual mode, he was a very attractive man.

Gracie cleared her throat and pasted on a smile. "Good morning. I'm so sorry to bother you, but my car won't start, and I have no idea what's wrong. It worked fine yesterday, and now I need to get to the animal clinic. Is there any way you could take a quick look?" She crossed her arms across her middle, as if bracing herself in case he said no.

With a slow nod, Blake ran his hand down his face and glanced behind him before facing her again. "I'll need to let the kids know what I'm doing. I never leave them inside alone."

"That sounds wise. Do you want me to stay with them?" Feeling more awkward than ever, she hoped that didn't sound too forward. After all, her neighbor hadn't been overly friendly.

He appeared to consider her offer, then shook his head. "No, that's okay. I'll tell them to stand in our yard."

Blake hurried away from the door, so Gracie headed back to her driveway. Curious voices sounded seconds later.

She circled to see Trixie and Max staring at her with puzzled expressions, so Gracie gave them a cheerful smile. "Hi, Trixie and Max. Your dad is going to check my car because it won't start." Both children nodded.

"Should I stay in your yard with them?" Gracie volunteered, sending up a quick prayer this wouldn't be an ordeal. She was sure Blake had other things to do.

"You could, even though they should be fine." He swiveled toward his children and told them in a kind but firm voice, "You both are to stay here in our yard. I'm only going to be in the driveway next door."

The driveway next door? Had he forgotten her name already? Gracie stretched to hand the car key to Blake, then joined the twins.

"Why won't your car work? Is it sick?" Trixie asked with the innocence of a young child.

Gracie released a sigh. "I hope my car isn't sick, sweetie. That's nice of your daddy to take a look." Before she could say more, Trixie spoke again.

"Our mommy was sick. Now she's in Heaven." She spoke almost matter-of-factly, but Gracie's heart broke at hearing this.

"I'm so sorry, sweetheart. I'm glad you have a good daddy to take care of you." Gracie was about to change the topic to animals when Blake jogged toward them.

"It's a dead battery, so I'll pull my car over to

your driveway and give you a charge. I have jumper cables. You should be good to go within fifteen minutes, hopefully."

"Thank you so much, and I'm sorry to trouble you."

With a hint of a smile, Blake responded. "It's fine." Then he instructed his children to remain there in the yard while he finished. As he hurried to get his cables, Trixie shyly reached up and took hold of Gracie's hand.

Gracie had the urge to embrace the child in a warm hug, but she didn't want to frighten her since they'd only recently met.

"What's your name? I forgetted." Trixie scrunched up her nose as if in thought.

"Miss Gracie. And I like your name, Trixie." Then she turned and grinned at Max. "I like your name too, Max." He ducked his head in embarrassment. It was obvious that Trixie was the outgoing one of the twins.

While Blake hooked up the cables and charged her battery, she continued visiting with the children, relieved that nothing else was said about their deceased mother. The conversation centered around Gracie's cats and her job at the animal clinic, and it seemed only minutes before her car was ready to go.

"Thank you. How can I repay you?" She needed to get to work but wanted to make sure her neighbor knew she was grateful.

Blake shook his head. "No problem. Thanks for staying here with the twins."

Trixie was still clasping Gracie's hand and

reluctantly let go when Gracie told them good-bye. "I have to go and help other animals who are sick, like Pedro was. But I enjoyed visiting with you both."

The twins waved as she hurried to her car, and when Trixie called out "Bye, Miss Gracie," her heart squeezed.

Ten minutes later she arrived at the animal clinic and rushed into the office. Even though she'd texted the receptionist to let her know she'd be late due to car trouble, the plump woman still appeared concerned when Gracie hurried in.

"Are you okay?"

She nodded, feeling a bit breathless. "Yes, what a blessing my neighbor had jumper cables and was able to help." She knew a heated blush was creeping up her face.

Dora's eyes widened. "Would that be the handsome neighbor with the adorable twins?"

"Yes, that's the one. I'm grateful he could help, or I'm not sure what I would've done." Gracie grabbed that day's client folders on the counter.

Reaching for a peppermint in a dish on her desk, Dora arched her eyebrows playfully. "How wonderful to have a neighbor who's not only handsome but able to help with car problems." She popped the striped candy into her mouth.

Gracie rolled her eyes, more than ready to get to work. But as she went about her day, her mind drifted back to her morning. Yes, Blake Donovan was certainly handsome, but why wasn't he friendlier? He wasn't rude to her, but he definitely didn't appear cordial, at least not with her. Maybe he was grieving his late wife and that affected his disposition. But Gracie had a soft spot for the children, so whenever she could do something for them, she would. Despite how guarded their father might be.

~ ~ ~

Why did he continue thinking about his neighbor? She'd needed help with her car, and he had been available. He'd done a good deed. That was all there was to it.

Yet when Gracie was standing close by, her presence caused his stomach to feel jittery, which was ridiculous. Sure, she had a pretty face with a sweet smile, and her long auburn hair was eye catching. Why should he care? Awkward memories of past dates flashed through his mind. There was no way he wanted to repeat those experiences, so it was much safer to avoid a relationship and focus on his priorities—the twins and his job.

His ringing cell phone jarred him, and he glanced at the caller ID, not recognizing the number. Probably a telemarketer. "Hello?"

An unfamiliar female voice came through, and realization dawned on him.

"Blake Donovan? This is Chantelle Dawson. Mr. Whitley said I could go ahead and contact you to arrange our meeting times." She paused, as if expecting Blake to jump in.

Keeping his tone professional, Blake replied

with the only words he could at the time. "Okay, what did you have in mind?"

"Well, Mr. Whitley said he'd like us to begin working together as soon as possible. Before I shadow you on appointments, I think we should meet in person. I'm staying with a friend in Destin, and Mr. Whitley said you live in Coastal Breeze, so what works for you?" At least she was trying to accommodate him, so that was a good sign.

"I'm not sure if Mr. Whitley told you, but I have young children and have to make childcare arrangements for them. Next week they'll be in a preschool during the day, but this week I'm at home with them." There. He'd let her know his situation, so maybe she'd be understanding.

"Mr. Whitley did mention your children. I'm eager to get started, so would it work if I came to your place for a brief introductory meeting?"

Wow, this woman didn't waste any time diving in. Blake hoped he wouldn't regret it, but he went ahead and agreed to her suggestion.

"Great. Which day this week works for you? And I'll need directions to your house."

Five minutes later the call was finished, and Blake had a sinking feeling in his gut. He didn't like this arrangement at all, but what could he do? Chantelle Dawson was coming to his house on Thursday, so he'd have to make sure the living room was tidy, and more importantly, he'd have to come up with some activities to keep the twins occupied while he met with the new employee.

Would his life keep getting more complicated? He knew things would be simpler if he wasn't a single parent. But he wouldn't allow his thoughts to go there. Besides, how likely would it be to find a woman willing to marry a man with two young children? And living in this small beach town didn't provide many opportunities to interact with women. Except his neighbor, and she most likely had a steady boyfriend or fiancé.

As if reading his thoughts Trixie exclaimed. "There's Miss Gracie!" His daughter pointed to the window beside the kitchen table where she sat having a snack with Max. Sure enough, Blake saw Gracie carrying grocery bags toward her door. His mind took off. She was probably planning on cooking a big dinner for her boyfriend. For some reason, that didn't lift his spirits. At all.

~ ~ ~

"I'm so glad I went to the store after work today, even though I was tired." Gracie told Kira as she balanced her phone on her shoulder. She switched on the oven for the cookies and hoped they turned out well.

"Well, I wish I was there right now to enjoy some of those cookies you're about to bake. Are you planning to share them with your coworkers?" Kira's unexpected question made Gracie pause. Her best friend could always tell from her voice if something was going on, so she may as well explain.

"Actually, I'm baking them for my neighbors. The single dad next door helped me with a dead battery, so to show my appreciation,

I thought he and his children would enjoy some cookies."

"Single dad? The same cute guy we saw when we got back from the restaurant?" Kira's voice held a hint of excitement, so Gracie knew she'd better play it down.

"Yes, that's the neighbor. Anyway, since he has young twins, I figured they might enjoy some homemade cookies. No big deal." Oh great, now Kira would likely read too much into this.

To Gracie's relief, her friend's favorite television show was about to start, so their call ended. But she'd better be prepared for a barrage of questions the next time they talked.

Soon the aroma of chocolate chip cookies wafted through her kitchen, and Gracie hoped they'd taste as good as they smelled. She'd already decided to wait until after work the next day to deliver them. Besides, the twins would probably be going to bed soon, so it wouldn't be a good idea to tempt them with a sugary treat before bedtime.

Thinking of Trixie and Max brought a smile to her face, but also sadness that they had no mother in their lives. They were so young.

Dark clouds billowed overhead as Gracie pulled into her driveway the next day after work. Most likely a storm was brewing, so she'd better deliver the cookies to her neighbors before she got caught in the rain.

Minutes later she clasped a foil-covered plate as she walked the short distance between the two houses. Children's laughter reached her ears as she stepped onto the porch. After tapping on the door,

Gracie realized her heart was pounding. What was wrong with her?

The door swung open and Blake's face registered surprise. He was flanked on either side by the children, who peered shyly up at her.

Extending the plate towards Blake, Gracie spoke cheerfully. "I baked some chocolate chip cookies and hope you and your children will enjoy them. It's just a little something to show my gratitude for your help with my car the other morning. I appreciated your help." Had her words tumbled out, or did she just feel that way due to her nervous state?

As Blake reached out to take the plate of cookies, a smile eased onto his face. Trixie piped up. "Miss Gracie, you cooked us cookies?" She rubbed her hand in circles on her stomach, and although Max remained silent, his eyes widened in anticipation.

"Yes, I did, Trixie. And I hope you all will enjoy them. They're chocolate chip, which is my favorite."

Blake was grinning—the first time Gracie had actually seen the man grin. "Oh yes, we all enjoy chocolate chip cookies. You didn't need to do this but thank you. We'll have some after supper." He winked at Max.

Trixie stepped toward Gracie and extended her small hand. "Miss Gracie, can you come in our house?"

This was totally unexpected, but Gracie managed a quick response as she gently squeezed the child's hand. "You're so sweet, but I only arrived home from work a few minutes ago and my kitties are waiting for their supper. They get very hungry while I'm at work."

With a nod, Blake thanked her again for the cookies before ushering his children into the living room. Gracie hurried back home, annoyed that her heart was still racing. So what if he was an attractive man? She needed to think of him as her neighbor. Period. Besides, up until today he'd never acted that friendly toward her. It took a plate of homemade cookies to coax a grin from the man.

Still, it gave her a warm feeling that she'd taken a treat to her neighbors, because seeing those young children always tugged at her heartstrings. The fact their father was good-looking didn't matter at all. *Yes, that's what I'll keep telling myself.*

~ ~ ~

Blake sat across from Chantelle Dawson at the kitchen table, hoping the twins would play well in their rooms. He didn't like this situation at all but reminded himself things should be easier when his children were attending the church preschool.

Chantelle smiled at him as she held her pen in ring-clad fingers. The woman apparently liked jewelry. It was hard to avoid noticing the abundance of gold chains and bangles she wore. Although nice, she was clearly a go-getter who wanted to take off in the company. In fact, one of the first comments she'd made after meeting Blake at his door was her desire to climb the ladder as quickly as possible.

Now she batted her eyelashes and grinned coyly. "I so appreciate Mr. Whitley pairing me up with you because I told him I want to gain as much knowledge and experience as possible."

Blake offered a polite nod and gestured to the forms spread out on his kitchen table. "I'll do what I can to assist you, but remember I've only been a representative for four years."

She released an exaggerated laugh and reached over to pat his arm. "Four years sounds like a lifetime to me."

For some reason, her laughter grated on his nerves, and he forced himself to stay focused on the information in front of them.

After almost an hour, he told Chantelle that was enough information for their first meeting. He handed her a copy of his appointments for the upcoming week. "My twins will be in a church preschool, so I'll try to do the majority of my work while they're attending that program."

Her eyes widened, and she reached out and patted his arm again—something else that grated on his nerves. "I know it must be difficult for you being a single dad, and your children are *so* cute." Was she sincere, or simply saying what she thought he wanted to hear?

Blake was more than ready for his new coworker to exit his house. "Yeah, they're really good kids. It was nice to meet you, Chantelle, and I guess I'll see you at the address on the schedule." He gestured to the sheet she grasped in her hand.

"Okay, I'll be there. Thank goodness for GPS or I'd get so lost trying to locate addresses." A sudden sharp peal of laughter almost caused Blake to jump.

He reached for the door, hoping she'd get the hint. To his relief she did, although it seemed she left reluctantly.

Peering out the living room window to make sure she'd left, he released a long sigh. He needed to give his children a treat, because they'd only interrupted once during his meeting with Chantelle, and that was resolved quickly, thanks to the chocolate chip cookies.

He grinned as he heard them running from their bedrooms.

"Is that lady gone?" Trixie furrowed her little brow.

"Yes, she's gone. I am super proud of you both for being good while I talked with her about work. And because I'm so proud of you, we'll go get ice cream soon." Seeing their faces light up caused a lump in Blake's throat. How easily delighted they were at this age, and he hoped as they grew older he could maintain a good relationship with them. For now, he didn't want to think about his job or Chantelle or anything else except spending time with his kids. But as his eyes landed on the plate of cookies from their neighbor, his mind jumped to Gracie and for some reason he couldn't explain, a calm and pleasant feeling fell over him. Strange, since he hardly knew her.

~ ~ ~

On Sunday Gracie hurried into the building to find a seat. Kira had messaged she had a sinus headache and wouldn't be attending, so Gracie took the nearest seat to enjoy the prelude music before the service began.

Many members of the congregation smiled at her and she recognized several familiar faces from the past few weeks. It amazed her that she was still new in this small community yet already felt at home here.

The preacher's message was inspiring and the choir's voices blended well, giving Gracie an uplifting sense of peace that morning. When the service ended, she headed toward the door with the others but heard a woman's voice calling to her.

"Honey, may I speak with you a minute?"

Gracie spun around and saw the woman who owned the local gift shop grinning at her.

"We chatted when you visited my shop, Ginny's Treasures by the Sea. I'm Ginny Grover."

Gracie smiled. "Yes, ma'am, I remember. I love your shop and plan to visit again soon." Did she want to tell her about an upcoming sale at the gift shop?

Ginny stepped to the side so as not to block the aisle, and Gracie followed suit. The older woman leaned in. "I wanted to ask if you'd help with our church festival in late October. Last year we had a summer festival and it was wonderful. But with hot weather in July, we decided to try a fall festival this year. My dear niece, Emma, is helping too, but she's expecting her baby in December, so I'm trying to make sure she doesn't overdo." Ginny paused, as if giving Gracie a moment to digest the information.

Why not? Gracie nodded. "Yes, I'll be glad to help in any way I can."

Ginny's face lit up. "Oh, that's wonderful, sugar! Thank you so much." She reached in her handbag and lifted out a sheet of paper containing details about the festival. "If you want to look over this at home and decide which area you'd like to help with, and also if you have any additional suggestions, please feel free to let me know." She reached up and fingered the lovely mosaic cross necklace she wore, obviously relieved that Gracie had agreed to help.

"Okay, that sounds good. And I'm Gracie Norton, by the way."

"Thank you again, Gracie. My phone number is on that sheet if you have questions, or most days you can find me at my gift shop." Her voice held a lilt.

After Gracie exited the church and headed to her car, she replayed her conversation with Ginny Grover. The woman was friendly and outgoing, so she was the perfect one to head up a festival. Not to mention, she exuded energy.

While eating her lunch, Gracie studied the festival information sheet. This might be fun. At least, it would be the perfect way to meet others in the community. And who knows—maybe her neighbor would bring his adorable twins to the festival. For some reason, the thought of the man next door caused her stomach to somersault. But she told herself it was only because she'd eaten her sandwich too quickly.

~ ~ ~

Blake was glad he'd taken the twins to visit the church preschool the previous Friday, because he felt it helped them—and him—not be so nervous. The three women who ran the program were friendly and welcoming, and after leaving the church, Trixie had asked him when she and Max could return.

Now as he drove the short distance to the Coastal Breeze Christian Church, he told himself that his children would be safe and happy in the program. Besides, he'd given his cell number, so the teachers could reach him if necessary.

"They'll be fine." The oldest of the three workers smiled warmly before turning her full attention to the twins.

Blake stood a few moments observing Trixie and Max as they peered at the other children in the preschool, and he knew this would be good for them. With a tightness in his stomach, he made himself head out the door to return home and get busy with work.

Thankful he wasn't being shadowed by Chantelle today, he realized he dreaded working with the woman. But since it was temporary, he could do this. He *had* to do this.

Around noon his cell phone rang so he pulled his attention away from the reports he'd been working on. His regional manager's upbeat voice came through, and for a few seconds, Blake panicked. Had he forgotten to do something?

"Hello, Blake. Ed Whitley here, just checking to see how things went with Miss Dawson."

"Hi, Mr. Whitley. It was fine. She'll be shadowing me tomorrow at my appointment in Destin." Blake worked to keep any negative tones from his voice.

"Great, great. I'm sure you two will get along very well. Who knows, Blake? Maybe a lasting friendship will develop from this working relationship." Mr. Whitley released a strong laugh, causing Blake's gut to tighten.

He had no desire at all to have a lasting friendship with the woman, and after their time of working together ended, she'd return to Orlando and that would be the last time he'd have to listen to that laugh. But he couldn't very well explain that to his manager.

The two men discussed the upcoming appointments and the company's plans for expansion to other southern states. Before the call ended, his boss commented. "Blake, thanks again for helping Chantelle. I really feel she'll be an asset to our company, and the fact you're training her is a big plus for you."

"Glad to help." That was the best he could do, and only hoped Mr. Whitley didn't hear the resentful tone in his voice.

When it was time to pick up the children from preschool, Blake decided on a whim to take Pedro along in the car. That would be an extra treat for the twins.

On the return drive home, Blake smiled as Trixie and Max both shared about their first day at the school, with Trixie doing most of the chattering as usual. But what a relief they seemed happy, because that would be a tremendous help with childcare, not having to worry about them.

As he turned into the driveway, Trixie asked a question that caught Blake off guard. "Daddy, when can we see Miss Gracie again? I like her."

"Well, she's our neighbor so I'm sure we'll see her again before too long."

"Can she eat supper with us sometime?"

Where was this coming from? Blake didn't understand why his daughter was so fascinated by the woman next door—especially since they'd only been around her a few times.

He calmly replied, "I'm sure Miss Gracie stays busy with her job and other activities. But I'm certain we'll see her again soon." He quickly changed the topic as he turned off the car. "We need to make sure Pedro stays with us, so hold tightly to his leash." Both children nodded as they shared the responsibility of grasping the dog's leash in their small hands.

Now to enjoy the remainder of the day with his children, because thoughts of working with Chantelle the next day hung over him like a dark cloud.

"Daddy, why do you have a frown?" Max's question jolted him as he fixed an afternoon snack for the twins.

Blake chuckled and shook his head. "I'm sorry, Max. I was thinking about work, but I should be smiling because you and Trixie had a wonderful day at your new school." He ruffled his son's hair, then told both twins to wash their hands and enjoy their snack.

That night after tucking both children into bed, Blake mulled over the upcoming day. Hopefully the appointment at the medical office would go smoothly. If only he didn't have such negative feelings toward his trainee, because their working relationship was temporary. All he had to do was maintain a polite demeanor and do the best he could while training her. Still, he'd be relieved when he didn't have to deal with Chantelle Dawson at all.

~ ~ ~

Chapter 3

"Oh honey, what a cute game!" Ginny Grover stopped at the table where Gracie constructed a simple game for the upcoming fall festival. The volunteers were in the church fellowship hall busily working on activities and Ginny stopped at each table to see if anyone needed supplies or help.

Gracie thanked her and noticed the cute pumpkin earrings Ginny wore. At that moment another worker called to her so Ginny scurried off. The woman was amazing—especially for her age. She owned and ran the town's gift shop and was very active in the church. Ginny's husband, Claude Grover, must rival his wife's energy level because he was always helping at the church too.

Gracie enjoyed this volunteer work more than she'd expected, and even though Kira was battling a cold and unable to help this morning, Gracie had shown up along with eight other workers to work on festival games. Since there were still three weeks until the event, things should be ready by then.

She surveyed some of the other colorful games and decorations being created around her. How excited children get over simple events like a church festival. The image of the twins living next door to her popped into Gracie's mind. They'd enjoy attending the festival, so hopefully their dad would bring them. Maybe she should mention it to him, just to make sure he knew about it.

Her heart fluttered as she thought of the handsome man next door. Was she looking for an excuse to speak with him? No! She genuinely wanted to make sure he knew about the festival, so he could bring his children.

An hour later the volunteers exited the fellowship hall as Ginny called out her thanks to each of them. Gracie drew in a deep breath of the ocean air and lifted her face to the sunshine. Even though she missed the trees with autumn colors at this time of year, she had to admit she loved living at the coast. More than she'd thought she would.

While she was out, she might as well head to the grocery store, then later she'd take a walk on the beach before dusk. Since Kira was sick, the two friends wouldn't be eating out as they often did on the weekends. A twinge of loneliness poked at her, but she refused to give in to her emotions. In time she'd meet more people, and maybe even start dating again. Yet she was in no rush for that after Derek.

Heading into the busy store on the outskirts of

Coastal Breeze, Gracie realized she'd not written a grocery list, but hopefully she'd remember everything she needed. With her household consisting of herself and two felines, her shopping list was never long. *Maybe one day I'll have a husband and children, and my list will be longer and my life busier. Add to that a small shelter to house abandoned cats and dogs.*

Ten minutes later she was almost finished in the store when she remembered the canned soup. Turning her cart around, she headed for the aisle with canned goods.

"Miss Gracie!" A vaguely familiar child's voice called out and she turned her head toward the voice.

Trixie ran up to her, smiling as her dark hair bounced on her small shoulders. Max trailed behind his sister, with Blake following with a shopping cart. His expression was polite, but not overly eager to see her.

"Hey there!" Gracie greeted the children warmly, then nodded at their father. Why did he seem so reserved around her? Maybe he was just preoccupied while trying to shop for groceries with two young children in tow.

Trixie gestured toward the cans of cat food in Gracie's cart and her eyes widened. "You have a cat, Miss Gracie?" Max edged closer and also peered into her cart.

"I sure do. I have two kitties and their names are Tubby and Cheddar. Tubby is gray and Cheddar is orange with stripes." Although she'd mentioned her felines before, she didn't expect the children to remember.

"Like a tiger?" Trixie seemed fascinated by this bit of information.

"That's right, Trixie. But Cheddar is much smaller than a tiger, and he's very sweet. So is Tubby. Maybe sometime you and Max can meet my cats—they don't go outside, because they're indoor kitties." A quick glance at Blake rattled her nerves since he hadn't joined in their conversation.

"Daddy, can we visit Miss Gracie's house and see her kitties?" Trixie lifted her gaze to Blake. Even Max looked expectantly at his dad.

"We'll see. Tell Miss Gracie good-bye so we can finish getting groceries and visit the beach." A hint of a smile played on Blake's mouth as he made eye contact with Gracie.

Both children said good-bye and hurried to their father's side—obviously eager to get to the beach.

Gracie called out good-bye and watched them walk toward the checkout line. Something tugged fiercely at her heart as she observed the twins. Those precious children…without a mother to love them. Blake was apparently a good father and spent time with them, and both children seemed well-adjusted. Still, it saddened her knowing they had no mother to spend time with them, tuck them in at night, and do all the special things loving moms do with their children.

Her eyes welled with tears, and she ducked her head while reaching into her handbag for a tissue. She'd better get a grip and finish her shopping, or she might encounter someone from church and they'd wonder what on earth was wrong with her. She continued toward the soup aisle, grabbing two cans and then hurrying toward the checkout line. She caught sight of Blake and the twins heading to their car, but she forced herself to focus on her groceries and getting her money ready to pay.

As she drove home, Gracie couldn't deny the pull of her heart toward the twins, and she again determined to do whatever she could for them. Even if their father was never overly friendly toward her, that didn't matter. She'd focus on Max and Trixie. And if Blake did become friendlier toward her, fine. If only her heart didn't race when he was near.

~ ~ ~

As Blake gripped Pedro's leash and watched his children laughing and kicking at the wet sand, his heart was filled with love. Moving to Coastal Breeze had been a blessing for them as a family. So why did an undercurrent of frustration hover just beneath the surface of his emotions? Maybe he needed a phone visit with Sarge. The older, wiser man had a knack for putting things in perspective and helping Blake see the overall picture.

"Daddy, look! Are those seagles?" Max's excitement and mispronunciation of seagulls brought a grin to Blake's face.

"Yes, son. Those birds are seagulls, and

they're looking for a fish to catch for their supper." The twins watched the birds in fascination. They enjoyed twenty more minutes on the beach before brushing the sand off, then climbed into the car for the brief trek home.

After reading bedtime stories to the twins that evening, Blake tucked the children into their beds. As he covered Trixie, she gazed at him with a slight frown.

"Daddy, our teacher said we need to come to Sunday School."

Surprised by her statement while trying to ignore the guilty prodding of his heart, Blake asked, "Why did your teacher say that?"

"Miss Katie teached us about Baby Jesus, and Kyle knowed about Jesus from Sunday School. Then Miss Katie said we all need to come like Kyle does." She eyed her father, obviously waiting for his response.

"I'm glad Miss Katie is teaching you about Jesus. See, you're learning a lot in your preschool." *Not the best reply, Donovan.* He didn't want Trixie to become upset, so he added a comment that seemed to satisfy her. "Maybe we can talk about Sunday School later." He placed a gentle kiss on her forehead and was relieved when she closed her eyes.

As he flipped through the channels on the remote, he kept thinking about Trixie's comments. Should he take the twins to church? How hypocritical Blake would feel doing that. But he wasn't about to tell his children that he and God didn't have the best relationship right now. No, even if the twins were older, he'd still feel rotten about sharing that.

Pushing the thought aside, Blake turned off the television and looked over his work notes. *Ugh.* He had to be shadowed tomorrow by Chantelle Dawson. Why did that woman irritate him so? Thankfully, she'd return to Orlando in a couple of weeks and then he wouldn't need to meet with her or be shadowed for appointments. Overall, she'd caught on quickly to her job responsibilities, but there was something disturbing about her mannerisms when it was only the two of them. She often touched Blake's arm and leaned in close to tell him something when they sat at a table. Was she flirting with him? Or maybe he was reading too much into her behavior. Either way, the bottom line was he would be very relieved when his trainee returned to her hometown.

~ ~ ~

"I'll be there for certain, Aunt Bonnie. I can't wait to see you and Uncle Fred again. We'll talk closer to Thanksgiving about the menu, because I plan on bringing plenty of food to help you out." Gracie had been happy when she'd received a phone call from her mother's sister, Bonnie. Even though she'd always been close to her aunt and uncle, the closeness deepened after Gracie's parents were gone. Moving far away from them had been the biggest challenge when accepting her job in Coastal Breeze, although Bonnie and Fred were completely supportive of her decision. Now they relied on phone calls a few times each month.

"Don't worry about the food because we always have more than enough. Since Fred's sister and brother-in-law are joining us, they'll be bringing food too. We should have a fun, noisy day." Bonnie laughed, the sound reminding Gracie of her own mother.

"I can't wait. Will I be able to see any of my cousins, too?" Gracie hoped Bonnie and Fred's three children would be joining them and was glad when her aunt happily informed her they'd all be there.

"Just be prepared to be bombarded by lots of questions. Everyone will be eager to know what it's like living at the beach." Bonnie laughed, and after a few more minutes of visiting, the call ended.

As she stepped to the kitchen sink to refill her cats' water bowl, Gracie caught sight of the twins playing in their backyard. Pedro ran and romped with them, and even with her doors and windows closed, Gracie could hear the happy squeals of laughter. *Those precious children.* She stood watching them for a few minutes, as if mesmerized by their carefree antics. Seeing Pedro running and fetching balls they tossed was an amusing sight, and for a moment she was tempted to head into her backyard and stand at the fence for a closer view. Yet if their father saw her, what would he think? That she was a pitiful spinster who had nothing else to do on a Saturday afternoon except watch the neighbor kids playing?

She turned away from the window, feeling an ache in her heart yet not sure why. Maybe she wanted a family of her own more than she realized. Sure, she was happy with her job and clung to her dream of having her own animal shelter. But she had to admit that deep down inside, she also longed for a husband and children.

Okay, enough serious thinking. Time for a walk on the beach. Ten minutes later she exited her car at the nearby parking area and headed down the short walkway to the water. Only a few beachgoers were out that afternoon and their voices were muffled by the surf and occasional squawk of seagulls.

Gracie stood still for a few minutes, gazing at the teal water with clusters of seafoam here and there. Today it reminded her of bits of sugary icing she used for cupcakes. That thought led her mind to the twins next door and how excited they'd been over the cookies she'd baked. They would surely enjoy a batch of her decorated cupcakes.

As if her thoughts had materialized, a child's voice rang out. "Miss Gracie!"

She spun to see Trixie and Max bounding toward her with Blake following behind, clutching Pedro's leash. The twins grinned, but their father appeared a little—perturbed? Why should he mind that his children were happy to see a familiar face on the beach? Her pulse sped up, but she made herself focus only on the sweet children now standing a foot away.

"Hello, Max and Trixie! Isn't it fun living so close to the beach?" She purposely kept her gaze trained on the little faces and did not meet Blake's eyes.

Their heads bobbed excitedly as Max pointed upward at two gulls soaring over the water's edge.

Trixie giggled. "Max likes those birds."

"They are fun to watch. See that one that swooped down to the water? He's trying to catch a fish for his supper." She stood close to the children as they pointed at the bird.

Blake's voice interrupted the moment. "Come on, kids. We need to let Miss Gracie enjoy her time on the beach." He wasn't gruff, but there was something in his tone that didn't sit well with her.

Raising her gaze to look directly into his dark eyes, she smiled sweetly. "They have added to my enjoyment. I was just getting some fresh air and exercise. I'm always glad to see Max and Trixie." She grinned down at them.

Suddenly Trixie reached out and grasped Gracie's hand. With a pleading voice, she turned to her father. "Can we walk with Miss Gracie? Please?"

Her heart melted as she gently squeezed the little hand that held onto hers. She didn't want to overstep and have her neighbor upset with her, yet it was fine with her if the twins joined her for a walk. No, it was *more* than fine. She'd thoroughly enjoy spending time with these eager children.

Blake hesitated as he sent a puzzled look to her, then shrugged. "I guess it's okay, if Miss Gracie doesn't mind." A hint of a smile broke through.

Turning toward the water's edge, Gracie held onto Trixie's hand as Max kept in step beside them. Blake followed a few feet behind. Every so often the small group stopped to examine a shell in the sand or watch the seagulls performing their aerial swoops and dives.

Gracie was filled with a happiness she'd not known in a long time. The simple act of walking on the beach with two precious, motherless children filled her heart with peace and joy. She also couldn't help wondering if others who passed them and smiled assumed they were a family. That thought made her smile—even if the possibility was remote.

~ ~ ~

"Daddy, that was fun. Can we walk on the beach with Miss Gracie every day?" Trixie tried to stand still as Blake combed through her freshly-shampooed hair. They'd returned from their beach walk, eaten sandwiches, and then each twin had a bath. Blake was amused at how excited his children had been over walking with their neighbor.

Of course, if he was honest with himself, he'd enjoyed the walk too, although he barely spoke two words to Gracie the entire time. Before they'd encountered her, his mind had been focused on his current job situation, so seeing his children happily chattering with their neighbor was a pleasant diversion. As he trailed Gracie walking between his twins, he was struck with the startling thought that to strangers they would appear a happy family. Two parents and two children enjoying an afternoon stroll on the beach with the family dog. His attention returned to Trixie, peering up at him as she awaited his reply.

"Sweetheart, I don't think we can walk with Miss Gracie every day. I'm sure she stays busy and besides, some days the weather isn't good and we can't visit the beach." As her little face appeared thoughtful, Blake's heart tugged. His kids needed a woman's attention at times, although he did his best as a single parent.

Playfully tweaking Trixie's nose, Blake grinned down at her. "I tell you what. I promise I'll do my best on the days when the weather is good and we'll visit the beach for lots more walks. Okay?" He hoped his words satisfied her.

She bobbed her head, then paused. "But can Miss Gracie walk with us sometimes?" He was learning his daughter could be quite persistent and hoped that wouldn't be a problem when she became a teen.

"I'm sure we'll see Miss Gracie again on the beach. So yes, you'll be able to walk with her again." Now to change the topic. Blake stepped over to the bookshelf in Trixie's room and gestured. "Why don't you and Max each choose a book and I'll read two tonight."

Thankfully there was no more mention of Gracie that evening, and soon two little drowsy heads were attempting to stay awake while their father read to them.

Later that evening his sister phoned and commented on the lovely church service she'd attended in Pensacola the previous Sunday and planned to visit again. Blake hoped she wouldn't scold him for not taking his children to Sunday School. To his relief, she didn't. Instead, Brianna asked when he'd need her to babysit again.

"I'm glad you asked, because there's an out-of-town trip coming up that my boss needs me to take. I really don't want to go, because I'll have to be away from the kids overnight. But according to my boss, this is a super important meeting and he made it sound as if I should be honored he asked me to attend." Blake released a wry chuckle.

Brianna teased him. "So, big brother, do you feel honored?"

"Not really." He was glad he and his sister could still tease as they had done when they were growing up. "Anyway, the trip is to Greenville, South Carolina, and it's in two weeks. Let me know if this interferes with your classes or you have other plans." He gave her the specific dates and was relieved when she assured him those dates should be fine.

"Don't know what I'd do without you, Bri."

"Yeah, I tried telling you that when we were kids, remember?" She went on to give him updates about their mother and her busy social calendar since she'd moved to Arizona.

"I need to phone her. We haven't talked

recently." A sliver of guilt ran through him, and he made a mental note to phone his widowed mother before the week was gone.

"Yes, you need to give her a call. She always asks about the twins too. She really misses them and hopes to see all of you over the holidays."

Blake would be certain to let his children speak to their grandmother—even a quick hello would be good.

When the call was coming to an end, his sister caught him off guard with a question. "When are you going to start dating again?"

"Excuse me?" He was teasing but needed time to compose a reply.

"You heard me, big brother. You're not getting any younger, and I'm sure there's someone special out there for you. Besides, your kiddos need a mom."

He cleared his throat, still grappling for a reply. "If you'll remember, I've dated a couple of women and those turned out to be big mistakes. When someone good comes along, then I'll ask her out. Until then, I'm fine being a single dad. But I appreciate your concern for me." He forced a chuckle, ready to end this conversation. Normally he never felt ill-at-ease when talking with his sister, but this topic wasn't one he cared to debate.

After the call ended he couldn't seem to shake Brianna's comments from his mind. As much as he didn't want to admit it, he knew she was right. His children needed a mom. But he wasn't about to start dating simply for the sake of finding someone who would step in and take over that role.

The image of his neighbor unexpectedly formed in his mind. Why did he think about her so much? Besides the fact his daughter seemed to adore her, Blake wasn't sure why he continued to have frequent thoughts of the auburn-haired woman. Yes, she was attractive, but so were lots of other women. He shouldn't think about her because he still knew little about her. Yet, he couldn't deny that he liked what he saw.

~ ~ ~

Gracie cringed as she looked at her caller ID. She almost slammed her cell phone back on the table and shuddered. There was no way she was going to answer a call from Derek. She had nothing else to say to him, and after the way he'd treated her, she didn't ever want to see him again.

Realizing her heart was pounding, Gracie leaned down and stroked the soft fur of Cheddar. She'd heard that stroking an animal's fur had been known to lower blood pressure, and at the moment she figured her blood pressure must be pretty high. She only hoped Derek wouldn't start phoning her on a regular basis. Maybe if she didn't answer he'd realize she didn't want to talk to him. *The creep. Leading me on while dating other women.* But that was in the past. Over.

A few minutes later her phone rang again

and she released a groan. When she hesitantly looked at the small screen and saw Kira's number, she breathed a sigh of relief. "Hey, friend. Whew! I'm glad it's you and not the creep."

"What? Has Derek phoned you?"

"He's tried to, but I didn't answer. I have nothing to say to him."

Kira's tone held concern. "He doesn't know where you live, does he? You sure don't want him to show up at your house."

"No, he just knows I moved to Florida. Hopefully no one back in Marietta has told him I'm in Coastal Breeze. He probably feels guilty for being such a jerk to me when we dated. But live and learn. I'm so over him."

"I know you are and I'm glad. He had issues—the main one being his self-centeredness. Ugh."

Gracie was again reminded how thankful she was to have Kira as a friend. *And* that they both now lived on the Florida panhandle, not too far apart.

"I phoned to see if you'll be at church tomorrow and if you'd like to eat out afterward."

"Yep, I'll be there. And that sounds good. You won't be with Craig tomorrow?" Gracie appreciated that her friend made time for her, even though engaged.

"No, he's going to help his parents do some work on their house. We had a breakfast date this morning, which was nice. I'll look for you at church and then we'll eat wherever you'd like."

The friends chatted ten more minutes before the call ended. Later that evening while doing laundry, her thoughts returned to Derek's call and her stomach tightened. As much as she fought the bad memories, now and then they came rushing back, like thorns pricking her finger. When they'd met at the animal clinic where Gracie worked north of Atlanta, Derek had been such a gentleman, showering her with gifts. But how quickly that changed. After he'd suggested she accompany him on a trip to Mexico he'd won at his job, Gracie had politely but firmly declined. There was no way she was traveling anywhere with him, not to mention the fact she was terrified of flying.

When he discovered her fear of flying, he ridiculed her, rather than showing compassion. After that, Gracie realized his true colors and began pulling away from him. As he demonstrated more immature, selfish characteristics, Gracie knew she must end the relationship. Once it was over, she had no regrets.

In retrospect she knew the Lord had certainly been looking out for her, because the position at the animal clinic in Coastal Breeze became available and she applied, thanks to Kira letting her know about the position. When she was accepted a week later, she made arrangements to relocate from her apartment north of Atlanta to the quaint beach community in Florida. Although she hated moving so far away from her aunt and uncle, Gracie was certain the move was the Lord's plan for her. It was a big step, but one she gladly took. It helped that Kira was already living in the general area, having moved to be closer to her fiancé.

Her eyes lit on a small framed photo of her parents, taken about a year before their accident. She smiled at the picture, knowing in her heart they'd be happy she moved to Florida and began a new life. As a peace settled over her, Gracie prepared for bed. Just as she was giving in to the heavy drowsiness, her phone rang. Reaching for her phone on the nightstand, she saw with dismay Derek's number on the screen. No way would she answer. Not tonight...or ever.

~ ~ ~

Blake was counting down the days until Chantelle Dawson would return to Orlando. He wasn't sure exactly what it was, but there was something about the woman that unnerved him. Her mannerisms, her voice, and the way her eyes bore into his as if trying to look into his thoughts. Some men might consider her attractive, but there was nothing about her that appealed to him.

After walking the twins into preschool on Monday morning, Blake drove to a medical facility on the outskirts of Destin, dread filling him the closer he came to his destination. Hopefully the appointment with the medical staff would go smoothly and then he could finish his day without Chantelle. But her tinny voice reached his ears upon arriving in the parking lot of the medical building.

"Good morning!" She practically gushed and strode toward him in a tight-fitting skirt and blouse.

Was it his imagination or were her perfume and makeup extra heavy today? When she placed her hand on his arm the moment she reached him, he stiffened, afraid she was going to pull him into a tight embrace.

"Good morning." He hoped his tone didn't betray his inner feelings toward her. "I'm hoping this appointment goes well. Then you can enjoy the remainder of your day—unless you have paperwork to complete."

She smiled up at him and shook her head. "No, I don't think I have any paperwork to do, but I was hoping you could join me for lunch today. I'll even treat."

The sinking in the pit of his stomach had nothing to do with the strong coffee he'd been drinking all morning. The last thing he wanted to do was eat lunch with Chantelle. Drawing in a deep breath, he pasted on a smile. "I appreciate the offer, but I've got a lot of work, and then I'll need to get my kids from preschool."

Her face fell and she conjured up a pout that Blake knew was forced, complete with her bottom lip poking out. It was almost comical, but he didn't dare laugh. What kind of woman was he dealing with here? Best to turn the focus back to their appointment.

"We'd better head into the building. Maybe we'll be able to speak with Dr. Winters rather than another staff member. Whenever possible, I prefer interacting with the doctors themselves. It's good to hear firsthand how they feel about a particular product." Blake wasn't even sure Chantelle was listening to his comments.

She shrugged as if what he'd said was no big deal.

Regardless of her attitude or behavior, he would do his best to follow through with this assignment of training her. But he'd be more than happy when he no longer had to deal with her.

After entering the pristine office, Blake approached the sign-in counter with Chantelle close beside him. *Too close.*

When the receptionist learned they were pharmaceutical representatives, she smiled apologetically. "I'm so sorry, but Dr. Winters was called in to assist with an emergency surgery this morning, but we're hoping he'll arrive here within the hour. You're welcome to sit in our waiting room if you're not in a big hurry. Then as soon as he comes in, you can speak with him before he begins his appointments. I've already phoned his patients and moved their appointment times to later in the day."

Blake really wanted to complete this appointment, so he may as well wait for the physician. Unfortunately that meant added time with Chantelle, but with any luck, she'd look at a magazine or watch the television mounted on the office wall.

He nodded at the receptionist. "Thank you. If you're sure it's okay, we'll just wait for Dr. Winters."

Since no patients had arrived, all the chairs in the waiting area were empty. Blake grabbed a sports magazine from a small table and sat in a chair. To his dismay Chantelle took the chair beside him.

While he pretended to be absorbed in an article about football, Chantelle studied her fingernails, crossed and uncrossed her legs, then released a frustrated-sounding sigh.

A few minutes later , she chattered about a restaurant she'd gone to the night before with her girlfriend. From her description the place sounded more like a bar than a restaurant, and the more she talked the more animated she became.

Blake attempted to pay attention to her, although he had no interest at all in what she'd done the previous evening. He didn't want to be rude, so he nodded now and then as he continued holding onto the magazine. Apparently, it didn't concern her that she might be interrupting his reading.

When the receptionist informed them the doctor had arrived and could meet with them, Blake felt like releasing a whoop of joy. He gathered his supplies and followed the receptionist through a hallway to the doctor's private office. Chantelle stayed close on his heels. When they reached the room, he gestured for her to enter first and be seated. He hoped she wouldn't try to be overly friendly with the physician, who was already behind on his day.

Twenty minutes later their meeting ended, and Blake was thankful Chantelle had remained quiet as he and the doctor spoke. After leaving samples and information sheets with the middle-aged man, Blake thanked him before he and Chantelle headed out.

"That went well. Do you have any questions?" He hoped she didn't, but if she did he'd answer them. After all, he *was* her trainer.

She shook her head before making her pouty face again. "No, except are you sure you can't have lunch with me?" She reached out a hand and touched his arm.

His gut tightened and he had to be careful not to jerk his arm away from her touch. "No, I'm sorry but I cannot. As I said earlier I need to catch up on some paperwork and make sure to get my twins on time from preschool. Since Dr. Winters was running late for our meeting, now I'll have even less time before I need to be at the preschool. You enjoy your lunch, though." He stepped away from her while he was still speaking.

Chantelle stood as if rooted to the spot, appearing shocked that he'd refused her offer. *Again.* The pout she'd had seconds earlier changed to a dumbfounded expression.

"Our next appointment will be Wednesday at ten o'clock. The location and details are on the sheet I gave you. Do you still have that?"

She nodded silently before heading to her car.

Relief washed over Blake when he reached his car. Yet in addition to relief he had a strange feeling that future meetings with his trainee would be awkward. He wasn't rude to her when he declined her lunch invitation, but his training procedures didn't include social outings with his trainee.

As he drove home to squeeze in some work before picking up the twins, he was certain of one thing. His time with Chantelle Dawson couldn't end soon enough.

~ ~ ~

The following Saturday Gracie spent several hours helping with festival preparations at the church. As she looked around at the various activities that would be offered for young children, she was again reminded of her neighbors, and the fact she needed to invite them to the festival. When she'd seen them on the beach the previous weekend, why hadn't she thought then to extend the invitation? That would've been the perfect opportunity to let Blake know about the festival and some of the activities that would be offered.

"Oh, honey, I appreciate your help so much." Ginny Grover smiled at Gracie and then shook her head. "I just can't believe the festival is only a week away. But I think we'll be ready. Are you still able to work at the festival for more than one shift if needed? I know that's a lot to ask but I want to be prepared." The older woman gave Gracie a questioning look as she fingered a small pumpkin charm on her necklace.

Gracie smiled and bobbed her head. "Absolutely. I'm more than happy to help, and hope there will be a good turnout for this event."

Ginny appeared relieved at her reply. The two women chatted a few minutes before another volunteer called to Ginny with a question.

As she finished assembling treat bags, Gracie again thought of the twins. If necessary, she'd go to their front door and invite them. Hopefully their father would be receptive. He was always so reserved, even distant. Maybe he was still grieving.

When she arrived home from the church, she gave her cats a treat and then changed clothes for a quick walk on the beach. Although she had to drive to the area where she always began her walks, she didn't mind because she was thankful to live so close to the ocean. Besides, the actual drive took less than three minutes, so she couldn't complain.

Now that October had arrived, there were even fewer beachgoers, although the weather was still mild. A crisp, salt-misted breeze blew in from the gulf and lifted Gracie's hair from her shoulders as she began her walk. Thoughts of Derek's recent phone call attempts invaded her mind, but she shoved them away and focused on the beauty stretching out before her. Today the water appeared a shade of turquoise, with a few frothy whitecaps here and there. The usual gulls swooped down to nab a fish. Watching them always amused her and Gracie never tired of viewing the scenery here in Coastal Breeze.

"Miss Gracie!" The now-familiar voice called to her and she whirled to see Trixie and Max running toward her, with Blake and a leashed Pedro following them.

"Hello there! We meet again on the beach." Her

heart warmed at seeing the precious children. She added a quick hello to their dad and stepped over to give Pedro a good rubbing behind his ears. "Do you enjoy the beach too, Mr. Pedro?"

Blake nodded in response about the dog as Trixie burst into giggles.

"What's so funny?" Gracie continued rubbing the dog, who obviously appreciated her attention.

"You called him Mr. Pedro. Like he's a man." Trixie giggled again and was joined by Max.

Gracie feigned a puzzled frown and looked at both twins. "Well, he's a four-legged man, isn't he?" She was eager to see the children's reaction to her silly question.

Both twins shook their heads, still giggling.

Trixie eyed Gracie and spoke as if actually explaining something to her. "No, Miss Gracie. Pedro is a dog."

Not wanting the children to think she was a nutcase—especially given the fact she worked at an animal clinic—Gracie decided to admit she was joking. "Yes, I know Pedro is a dog. I was only kidding with you all." Suddenly she remembered her plan to invite them to the festival, so she turned her attention to Blake. For a few seconds it was difficult to concentrate on her words since she was acutely aware of his good looks. His light blue shirt accentuated his dark wind-tossed hair. With one hand holding the dog's leash and his other hand in a pocket, he reminded Gracie of a model posing in a catalog.

Focus, Gracie. She pasted on a wide smile as she gazed up at Blake. "I'm glad I ran into you all again, because I need to mention something to you."

His brows raised in curiosity and a polite partial-smile formed on his lips. "Yes?"

She proceeded to tell him about the church festival and how much she thought the twins would enjoy the activities. "I'm one of the workers, and each Saturday when I help prepare the games and prizes, I always think about your children and how much fun they'd have. If it's okay with you, I'd love for them to attend."

Both children stopped playing in the sand and were listening to her. Oh no—what if Blake was *not* okay with them attending the festival, and she'd made a big mistake mentioning it in front of them?

To her surprise Blake's partial-smile grew into a full smile and he nodded. "Yeah, the twins attend preschool there at the church, so I've already received information about it. I was planning to take them for a little while that Saturday, so now hearing you talk about it lets me know that they'd really enjoy it."

Gracie released a breath of relief. "Great. Hopefully the weather will be good that day for the outdoor activities, but even if it's not, there will be plenty of indoor games and fun. Not to mention a snack bar."

Trixie began hopping from foot to foot. "Daddy, we get to go to the festival?" She peered up at him with her small hands clasped.

He playfully ruffled her hair. "Yes, Trixie, you

and Max can go to the festival. But it's not today, so don't be too excited just yet."

"Miss Gracie, can you walk with us like you did that other time?" Trixie had already reached out and grabbed her hand.

"I sure will, if you're going to walk a little longer."

So once again the four of them—plus Pedro—strolled along the sugary sand as the water lapped at their feet. And Gracie was again reminded of the fact that to a stranger, they would appear as a family. And for some reason that thought appealed to her more than it had before.

~ ~ ~

PATTI JO MOORE

Chapter 4

Sunday morning arrived with rain and gusty winds, making Blake very thankful he'd taken his children to the beach the previous day instead of waiting until today. As he cooked oatmeal for Trixie and Max, Blake thought about their beach walk. The twins were excited to see Gracie again and have her join them on their walk. As much as he tried to deny it, he was glad to see the attractive neighbor. Which concerned him, because he didn't want or intend to be attracted toward her. That could be a big mistake. If they had a disagreement, things would be awkward whenever he saw her. As if she'd ever be interested in him anyway. She probably had a man in her life—someone from out of town.

As if reading his thoughts, Trixie entered the kitchen and gazed toward Gracie's house. "Daddy, when can we see Miss Gracie again?" Why was his child so taken with their neighbor?

He set their bowls of oatmeal on the table. "I'm sure we'll see her again soon. Please tell Max to wash his hands so we can eat our breakfast. Then you both can watch the new movie while I do some work." He tried to limit their television viewing, but sometimes Blake played a DVD of a cartoon movie so he could have uninterrupted time to focus on work.

During the afternoon the rain slacked off, but things were too wet to go outside. Blake was glad his children could entertain themselves with their toys and puzzles. They'd already viewed a cartoon, so that was enough television for a while. "I have an idea. Why don't you each build a house with the blocks? Then when I'm finished with my work, you can each tell me about the house you built." A simple idea but it worked.

As Blake returned to his work, his cell phone rang, showing Sarge's name on the caller ID. It wouldn't hurt to take a break while the twins were occupied with their blocks.

"Hello, my buddy. How are you and those precious twins doing?" Sarge's booming voice came through and Blake could visualize his friend sitting in his recliner while Nora bustled around in the kitchen. He missed them both and was determined to take his children for a visit before long.

"We're doing well, Sarge. It's raining here today, so the kids are playing inside and I'm hoping to get ahead on some work." He hesitated before saying what was on his mind. "Remember a while back when I mentioned changing jobs? What do you think?" He valued and trusted the older man and knew Sarge wouldn't advise him to do anything foolish.

"Blake, I think you should do what will make you the happiest as long as you can provide for your twins. Do you have any specific ideas yet?"

"Not really, and that's the problem. I can't give my notice with the drug company until I have something definite lined up. But with each passing week, I become more certain that I need to do something else. I'm thirty years old so if I'm going to change careers, I need to go ahead before I get much older."

Without hesitation his friend replied. "Then that's what you need to do. The type of work that interests you and provides for your children is the path you need to take. You'll never know unless you locate the one that's right for you."

Unable to keep from chuckling, Blake responded to his wise friend. "Yes, Sarge. You're always right."

An amused laugh came through the phone. "That's what I try to tell Nora, but she doesn't believe me."

Blake could picture Nora hearing her husband's end of the conversation and shaking her head. The woman must be an angel with the patience of Job.

"Seriously, Blake, pray about it. Now I know you don't want me saying that, but I have to speak from my heart. I'm sure not a saint but I do know I'd be lost without the Lord's help in my life all these years. Anyway, let me know what you decide to do, and you know I'll support you in any way I can. Including keeping the twins for a few days if you need to schedule some interviews. Nora would love having them here. But they'd come home spoiled rotten, just to let you know ahead of time."

What would Blake do without this wonderful couple in his life? He thanked Sarge for his advice and the men visited a little more, discussing the upcoming holidays and the current football season. After the call ended, Blake replayed Sarge's comments in his mind. His buddy had told him to do what he'd be interested in as long as he could support his children. Which meant he had some serious work to do investigating his options.

Max tugged at his sleeve to say he was hungry, so Blake headed into the kitchen to prepare a snack. But the remainder of that day, whenever he thought about finally taking steps to change careers, his heart lifted. And it also kept negative thoughts about Chantelle Dawson at bay, which was a blessing in itself.

~ ~ ~

Saturday arrived with sunshine and slightly cool temperatures—perfect weather for a fall festival. Gracie could feel the excitement in the air as she arrived early that morning to help with last-minute preparations.

Ginny Grover scurried around checking on each

area, exuding a positive spirit. The woman was amazing, and Gracie only hoped she'd have half that much energy when she was Ginny's age.

At that moment Ginny rang a little bell to get everyone's attention. "Welcome, friends, and thank you all so much for your help. The festival will officially begin in only thirty minutes, so please make sure your activity is all set to go. If anyone has a question or a problem please see me or my husband, Claude Grover." She gestured proudly to the older man standing a few feet away from her. He nodded at the crowd of volunteers.

"One more thing. Since we have lovely weather today, the hayride will run, so that's very exciting. The schedule is posted by the main door, so if any attendees ask what times the wagon is running, just direct them to that sign. We are so grateful to our own Midge Weatherbee for asking her nephew to provide the tractor and wagon. And the hay, of course." Ginny giggled before concluding her talk. "Most importantly, we want everyone to have fun today. God bless you all." With a wave of her manicured hand, Ginny turned her attention to her husband, apparently giving him a job to do because he headed to stacks of boxes along one wall and began moving them to various activities.

Gracie saw the box labels and knew they contained prizes for the games and activities. She'd overheard a volunteer commenting earlier that Ginny made certain each child took home plenty of prizes—many of them bearing an inspirational message or Bible verse.

Just then Ginny breezed over to her with an apologetic smile. "Gracie, do you mind helping at the fish pond? One of the workers phoned a few minutes ago and she's sick. I told her not to worry because we've got it covered."

"That's fine. I'm happy to help wherever needed." Gracie knew how important festivals were to young children, having helped with a few at her former church in Georgia.

Ginny reached out and patted her arm. "Oh, you're a peach." She scurried off to check on other activities.

Being new in the church, Gracie hoped to meet some members while helping with the festival. As she joined a thirty-something woman at the fish pond, squeals of delight met her ears as the first arrivals entered the large fellowship hall.

"Get ready—they're here!" Her coworker laughed and extended a hand. "Hi, I'm Livvy Burgess and I appreciate your help. My friend Ava got a stomach bug, so I insisted she stay home and rest. Besides, we don't want to get sick." Livvy shuddered and grinned.

"Nice to meet you. I'm Gracie Norton, and I'm happy to help."

Before the two women could continue their conversation, several excited children approached their activity. "How does this work?" A little boy who appeared to be around seven gazed up at both women.

Livvy explained. "You'll put the fishing pole

into the little pond and try to catch a fish. When you've hooked a fish, lift it out and see what number is painted on the fish. That's the prize bucket number you'll choose from. You get to pick out two items from that prize bucket."

Gracie watched the children as they listened, and her heart warmed at seeing them eager about such a simple activity. She'd heard comments from parents of older children who came into the animal clinic complaining about their kids getting bored easily, which she thought was a shame. She'd always found plenty to do when she was growing up, and even now couldn't imagine ever being bored.

The time passed quickly, and the two women visited between participants at their game. Livvy and her husband had two children and lived between Coastal Breeze and Destin.

"Miss Gracie!" The now-familiar child's voice called out as Trixie, Max, and Blake approached her.

Gracie didn't miss Blake's look of discomfort as he glanced around nervously. The twins' eyes darted from one activity to another, obviously ready to join in the games and fun.

"Hello, Trixie and Max. Would you like to go fishing in the little pond?" She gestured toward the child's wading pool that had been filled with water and contained colorful plastic fish.

Trixie peered up at her father. "Can we, daddy?"

Blake nodded and offered a guarded smile in

Gracie's direction.

She hoped he wouldn't rush the children at the festival simply because he felt uncomfortable. What could she do to ensure the twins had a good time? On a whim, she stepped closer to Blake.

"If you have errands or work to do, I'll be glad to keep the twins with me for a while. Another worker is coming to replace me in about ten minutes, so after that I could walk around with them while they enjoy the games and activities."

Surprise registered on his face as he seemed to be searching for a reply. Both children gazed up at him, and Trixie tugged on his arm as if urging him to accept Gracie's offer.

He cleared his throat and fixed his eyes on Gracie. "I appreciate that, but if you're working here today, you don't need to be babysitting my children."

Had he not heard that another worker was replacing her soon? Gracie increased the volume of her words and leaned closer, catching the musky scent of his cologne. "When the other worker arrives here for the fish pond, then I'll be free to take the children around to other areas of the festival. But if you're able to stay here a while with them, that's fine. I just wanted to offer so they can enjoy the activities." She didn't want to sound sarcastic, but the bottom line was she wanted the twins to have a fun time today. Whether their father was with them or not. She folded her arms across her chest, her chin lifted.

A shadow of relief passed over his handsome features and he slightly shrugged. "Okay, if you're sure you don't mind. I'll stay here until you're finished with your time, then I'll head home to do some work. When should I be back to get them?"

As happy as she was about his reply, Gracie was also a bit shocked that he was going to leave his twins in her care. Apparently, he trusted her more than his demeanor indicated. Or maybe he just wasn't a friendly man, and it wasn't anything against her. She smiled up at him. "I think about three hours would be good, if that's agreeable with you."

Blake nodded before leaning down to explain to the children that they'd be staying with Miss Gracie for a while at the festival. Although Max looked a tiny bit unsure, Trixie bobbed her head with confidence. "That'll be fun!" Her attention was immediately diverted to a nearby table with face-painting.

Gracie completed her shift at the fish pond as Blake and the twins strolled around the festival, stopping at several games to observe. Trixie's excited face squeezed at her heart, and she determined to make sure these precious little ones had a wonderful time while they were in her care this afternoon.

Although Blake offered to leave some money with her for the twins, Gracie politely but firmly refused. This was going to be her treat. And she'd enjoy every minute of it.

The next three hours flew by as she took her charges to various games, where they collected prizes that brought lots of smiles. After purchasing hot dogs, chips, and drinks at the snack bar, Gracie led the twins to one of the picnic tables set up outside. As the breeze blew in from the nearby gulf, both children squealed and giggled when their paper plates almost floated off in the wind. Gracie found herself laughing as much as the children and couldn't remember when she'd felt so carefree.

For the grand finale of her time with the twins, she accompanied them to the hayride. After only a few minutes they climbed aboard the long wagon, pulled by a tractor. Gracie remembered that Midge Weatherbee's nephew was in charge, so he must be the driver of the tractor. Although she didn't know Midge well, she'd been around her at church and was amused at the older woman's spry personality. *And* her attempts at matchmaking. Hopefully, she wouldn't volunteer to introduce Gracie to her nephew.

Thankful she remembered to keep her phone handy, Gracie snapped photos of the twins at various activities. Now she asked a teen boy seated across from them to snap a photo of her and the twins. They had straw in their hair, but that added to the giggles when they looked at each other.

When the hayride ended, the children were still laughing as they brushed their clothing. "That was fun, Miss Gracie!" Trixie clasped her bag filled with prizes and candy, and Max nodded in agreement at her words. His little hands gripped his prize bag. Since Blake hadn't given Gracie any stipulations about what the children could or couldn't have, she was sending them home laden with souvenirs of the church festival, in addition to pink and blue cotton candy.

As soon as the three of them stepped away from the wagon, Blake strode toward them, wearing a grin that made him even more attractive. Gracie tried to ignore the fluttering sensation in her heart.

"We had fun, Daddy!" Trixie waved her arms in the air to indicate they'd enjoyed most all of the activities. Then she proudly held up the bag containing her prizes. Max also chimed in, waving his own bag of prizes.

Blake ruffled Max's hair, tweaked Trixie's nose, and then offered a smile to Gracie. "So I take it things went well?"

"Absolutely. Your children were great and I think they had a fun time. I know I sure did." At that moment Gracie realized she didn't want to say good-bye to the precious little ones standing beside her.

"I can tell they enjoyed themselves. What do you tell Miss Gracie?" Blake eyed the twins with a hint of seriousness.

"Thank you, Miss Gracie." Max and Trixie spoke in unison.

On a whim, Gracie leaned down and gave each child a gentle hug. Then she smiled at them, lowering her voice as if telling a secret. "Thank you for enjoying the festival with me. I had a lot of fun." They both nodded, then Trixie surprised her by reaching out for another hug. Gracie's heart melted as she fought tears.

Watching Blake lead the twins to his car,

Gracie was again struck with how much she cared about Trixie and Max. It was obvious they were being raised by a father who loved them. Still, young children needed a mother's touch. Would the Lord somehow use Gracie in their lives? The unexpected thought sent her emotions into overdrive, and the tears she'd kept at bay now trickled down her cheeks.

Festival attendees swarmed around her, laughing and rushing from one activity to another. She should check and see if she was needed to work at any of the games or booths before heading home. At that moment Ginny rushed up to her and must've noticed the tears. "Oh, sweetie, are you allergic to that straw on the hayride? I've heard several folks here today commenting they'd love to ride in the wagon except for all that straw." She smiled but there was concern in her eyes.

Gracie forced a smile and shrugged. "I didn't think I was allergic, but something made my eyes water." She reached into her shoulder bag for a tissue, relieved that Ginny seemed to accept her explanation for the tears.

"Am I needed at any other activities this afternoon? I won't go home if you need me to work. Looks like everyone is enjoying themselves."

Ginny still eyed her closely and then patted Gracie's arm. "I appreciate all your hard work and help, sugar. The festival ends in about another hour so you're free to head home. You take care of those sniffles." The smile she sent Gracie conveyed the message that no matter what caused the tears, it would be okay.

Surprised at the tiredness that washed over her, Gracie hurried to her car. Gray clouds gathered overhead. The beautiful weather they'd had for the festival would likely be ending soon, but at least, most of the day was perfect for the outdoor activities.

Throughout the remainder of the weekend, her time with the twins continually came to mind. The laughter and excitement on their faces only confirmed the fact she'd love to be a mother someday. If only she'd be blessed with children like Trixie and Max, because they had captured her heart.

~ ~ ~

On Sunday evening Blake prepared clothes and snacks for the upcoming week. How tired his children had been after the Saturday festival, but at least that meant they were content to play indoors on Sunday while he accomplished a bit of work. He didn't get much done, though, because he kept seeing the image of Gracie flanked by his children on the hayride. Something about the way his kids looked up at her and laughed—not to mention Gracie's natural beauty—presented a picture of a sweet family. Yet that was ridiculous. Gracie wasn't part of their family. But there was no denying his twins adored her. *She's growing on you too, Donovan.* The silent voice reminded him of what he tried to ignore. His neighbor was not only attractive and kind, but she held appeal for each of them, himself included.

He looked over his schedule for the week ahead and his spirits took a nosedive. Two more meetings with Chantelle before she returned to Orlando. Whenever he thought about his trainee, he tensed. Blake wished the woman didn't affect him in such a negative way, but she did.

Monday morning, he accompanied the twins into the preschool building. As they stepped inside the hallway leading to the classrooms, an older woman approached them, clutching an empty platter, and grinned at his children. Trixie immediately exclaimed. "Hey, Miss Midge!"

The woman leaned toward Trixie and winked, then gave Max another wink. "How are my favorite twins this morning?" She wore a dark green shirt with autumn leaves stitched on the front, and she had dangling leaf earrings that swayed as she moved her curly gray head.

Max smiled shyly but Trixie spoke up. "We're good. Did you bring treats?" His daughter was eyeing the empty platter.

"I sure did, sweet girl. Cinnamon muffins and homemade applesauce, waiting for you children in Miss Katie's office." She shifted her gaze to Blake. "I'm Mildred Weatherbee, but my friends call me Midge. I like to bake goodies for the kids twice a week."

Blake's eyes crinkled. "That's a nice thing to do," then added, "I'm Blake Donovan, Trixie and Max's father. It's nice to meet you, Mrs. Weatherbee."

The woman frowned, and for a few seconds, he wondered if she might hit him with her platter. But then her frown turned to a playful smile and she pretended to scold him. "No, no! It's Midge to my friends, and since you're the father of these adorable twins, I'll consider you a friend." She hesitated only a few seconds before continuing. "I noticed your children at the fall festival on Saturday with that lovely Gracie Norton. Are you two dating?" Midge peered up at him innocently, as if her question was perfectly natural.

Uh oh. Blake could feel his face heating in a blush, and his twins were looking up at him. He shook his head. "No, we're neighbors, and she offered to take the children around the festival while I did some work at home."

"Oh, I see. Well that was so kind of her, but in the short time I've observed Gracie here at the church on Sundays, she seems like an angel." The older woman's eyes twinkled.

Blake needed to be on his way, and certainly didn't want any more questions from this well-meaning but somewhat bold elderly lady. "Nice to meet you, Midge. I'd better take the twins into their classroom and get to work."

For a second he was afraid Midge might continue talking, but to his relief she told them good-bye and headed out the door.

Minutes later as he drove to his first appointment at a medical facility in Shalimar, Blake replayed Midge's comments. She was quite taken with Gracie. His neighbor's charms had captivated everyone from his young children to an elderly church member.

Yet again he wondered why she wasn't married. Someone so pretty and caring and admired by others would surely have a beau, wouldn't she?

~ ~ ~

Monday morning was nonstop at the animal clinic, with clients bringing their pets to be seen for checkups and sickness. Finally around two o'clock Gracie stepped into the breakroom to grab a cup of coffee and catch her breath. As she sipped the warm brew, she was reminded of why she loved her job. Seeing the sweet cats and dogs brought in— especially if they weren't seriously ill or injured— always made her smile. It also reaffirmed her goal of having a small shelter for animals someday. *Someday.* Would her someday ever arrive? Marriage, children, and housing abandoned animals all remained on a list of goals that didn't seem any closer to being realized than it had a year ago.

"What's wrong, Gracie? Are you not feeling well this afternoon?" Dr. Tatum stepped into the breakroom.

Setting her coffee cup on the counter, she mustered a smile. "I'm fine, Dr. Tatum. Just thinking about our appointments today. Sometimes I wish I could take all the animals home with me." Well, that was the truth after all. But there was no way she was admitting that she'd been reflecting on her single status, even though her boss was a fatherly figure.

"Yes, I know what you mean. That's the downside of working with animals. There have been more than a few I've wanted to keep for myself." He sighed and shrugged. "But as long as I have a good feeling about the pet owners, then it's okay." Dr. Tatum poured himself a cup of coffee and checked his cell phone.

Gracie took the last swig of her coffee and washed out the mug at the sink, then made sure the exam rooms were ready for the remainder of that day's clients. She also needed to check the clinic's small laundry room. It was amazing how quickly blankets and towels used for the animals built up.

On her way home that afternoon, she decided to stop by the gift shop in Coastal Breeze. Aunt Bonnie's birthday was the following week, and although Gracie would see her at Thanksgiving, she wanted to mail a gift to arrive on her aunt's special day. She'd only visited the shop a few times, but each time she enjoyed browsing and seeing the unique assortment of gifts that owner Ginny Grover had for sale. A few minutes later she pulled into a parking spot for *Ginny's Treasures by the Sea* and noticed a few other cars parked as well.

The bell tinkled over the door as Gracie entered, and her nose was greeted by a pleasant cinnamon aroma that was perfect for the autumn season. Ginny strolled toward her, holding some Thanksgiving decorations. "Come in, Gracie. So good to see you. Have you recovered from working at our fall festival?" Ginny's southern drawl was followed by an easy laugh.

Gracie smiled. "Yes, ma'am. I really enjoyed helping with the festival and it looked like everyone attending had a good time."

The older woman nodded in agreement. "I noticed you were helping with some cute little twins at the festival. Later I saw an attractive man picking them up, and I assumed he's their father." She paused as Gracie again nodded. "Are you dating him? I secretly hoped you were." Ginny giggled as if she'd let something slip.

A warmth covered Gracie's face and she shook her head. "No, they're my next-door neighbors, and I offered to spend time with the twins while their dad did some work on Saturday."

Ginny appeared to be about to comment again, but two customers approached the counter, so she simply smiled at Gracie before scurrying to the cash register.

With her aunt in mind, Gracie began perusing shelves with nautical-themed gifts, including some small lamps she was certain her aunt would like. Although reluctant to be questioned by the well-meaning shop owner, Gracie didn't want to rush through shopping for the special gift. So she continued browsing, relieved when more customers entered the store keeping Ginny occupied.

After ten minutes, Gracie returned to the original lamp she'd eyed and carefully lifted it from the shelf. Then she spotted a small painting of a lighthouse, signed in the corner with the name of Avril. Hmm...had a local painted this? It was lovely.

When she stepped to the counter to pay, Ginny beamed when she saw the items being purchased. "I love these little decorative lamps, and even purchased one for myself." She gently placed the lamp in a bag, then gestured to the lighthouse painting. "I'm so happy you bought this painting. Avril, the artist, lives in Alabama, but her brother Thomas is married to my niece, Emma." With a chuckle she added. "Did you catch all that or have I confused you?"

Gracie assured her she wasn't confused a bit. "Thank you for explaining who the artist is—I was curious if she's a local resident. I'm sure my Aunt Bonnie will love both these gifts." She handed the money to Ginny, then inquired about her niece's pregnancy.

Ginny was beyond excited about the expected baby in December. "Since Emma's mother has passed away, I'll be like a grandmother to the child. Which means I can spoil the baby." As they both laughed, Gracie couldn't help but think what a blessed baby that would be. Then Ginny's brow furrowed. "I only hope that Thomas will get some help with his workload so he'll have more time at home. His job keeps him much too busy." She shook her head, then brightened and told Gracie to please visit her shop anytime.

While wrapping her aunt's presents that evening, Gracie replayed Ginny's question about Blake. Was it just a casual inquiry, or had Gracie's face given away how attractive she found Blake Donovan? She'd never been good at concealing her emotions. Sure, the man was handsome, but he'd shown no interest in her. None. In fact, they'd have had no interaction at all if not for the twins. At the thought of Max and Trixie, her heart squeezed. Why did those children have such an effect on her when she wasn't related to them?

There was something special about those precious little ones next door, and she'd continue doing whatever she could for them. Even if their father remained indifferent toward her, she would lavish attention on the twins. They'd stolen her heart, and she didn't mind at all.

~ ~ ~

Blake couldn't believe this was happening. On Thursday afternoon he'd arrived home with the twins, given them a snack, and looked over some paperwork. Minutes later his boss phoned with a disturbing call about Chantelle Dawson. Apparently she was upset or was offended that Blake wouldn't go to dinner with her, so she'd fabricated ridiculous stories—lies—about him to their boss. As he rubbed his throbbing temples Blake told himself this was a bad dream and he'd awaken soon. But no, his boss continued questioning him. To make matters worse, the man didn't believe Blake. Knowing it was time to be straightforward with his boss, he forged ahead.

"Mr. Whitley, I give you my word. I've done nothing inappropriate toward Miss Dawson. In fact, she's approached me more than once about going out with her, and I've politely declined. The first time I said no, she didn't seem pleased, but the next two times, she acted almost hostile." Blake took a deep breath.

"I have continued doing my best to help her learn the ropes in our company, but that doesn't include seeing her on a personal level, because I have no intention of dating Chantelle Dawson." There. He'd said it. Because from the beginning of this trainer/trainee relationship, Blake had a sneaking suspicion that Ed Whitley was playing matchmaker, and he had no intention of dating her. Aside from the fact the woman was definitely *not* his type. Not that he even knew what 'his type' might be these days. Right now his priority was caring and providing for his precious children.

Mr. Whitley responded after a few seconds, "I'll admit I really didn't think you, of all people, would be guilty of inappropriate conduct, but when a female employee makes an accusation, we have to follow up. Now, you're absolutely certain you didn't say or do anything at all that Chantelle Dawson might misconstrue as making advances toward her?"

Although Blake had never experienced blood pressure problems, he had a feeling his blood pressure reading must be through the roof. After a slight pause, he formed his words carefully. Nothing productive would come from lashing out or speaking in a disrespectful tone. After all, Mr. Whitley was still his boss.

"Mr. Whitley, I promise you that I have not

said or done anything to give Miss Dawson grounds for accusing me. I've been patient with her—going over details and asking if she had more questions—trying to make her feel confident in her position with the company since she's new. And when I've declined her invitations to go to bars after work, I've done it politely." What else could he say? Surely his boss believed him, but if not, there was nothing else to say. Maybe this was another sign that it was time to change careers.

Speaking in an apologetic tone, Mr. Whitley's words eased Blake's anxiety. "I'm sorry for the nature of this call, but I had to follow up. Tomorrow is your last day with Chantelle, so I'm hoping it goes smoothly. Then she'll return to her home base of Orlando and you'll not need to have further contact with her. I'll make sure to notify her manager in Orlando about this incident in case she attempts this with any employees there. Hopefully she won't. Maybe she decided you were worth pursuing and didn't like it when you turned her down." A light chuckle followed before his tone turned serious again. "Anyway, I do want to thank you for the training you've done with Chantelle. This looks very good in your records with the company."

Once the call ended, Blake pushed thoughts of Chantelle and her accusations from his mind or he'd be in a foul mood with his kids, and that wasn't fair to them. Yet his boss's words about the training making him look good almost made him laugh. Because Blake knew for certain that he had no desire to continue with the pharmaceutical company. The sooner he could break away and begin a new career, the better. The only problem was—what career should he pursue?

~ ~ ~

Friday morning Gracie scurried around the animal clinic, thankful that Dr. Tatum was again letting the staff leave early that day. She was eager to get home and do some baking, because Kira and her fiancé Craig were planning to visit the following day. Kira had volunteered Craig to do some yardwork for Gracie while the two women visited.

The next morning Gracie surveyed her home, making certain things looked neat and tidy. Although she was a clean person, at times clutter took over and made her house appear messy. She and her cats were fine with it, but whenever guests were coming she made sure to pick up. She'd baked brownies and a pecan pie and planned to brew a fresh pot of coffee when her company arrived.

Around one o'clock Tubby's ears perked up toward the front door. Her guests were here. She giggled as both cats made a quick run for her bedroom to stay safely underneath her bed. Stepping to the door, she swung it open to greet the couple.

"Mmm…something smells wonderful. Did you bake goodies?" Kira's eyes sparkled as she eyed her best friend.

"I sure did. Brownies and a pecan pie. A fresh pot of coffee is brewing too."

Craig grinned and patted his stomach. "Did Kira mention I work for food?" He laughed as Kira rolled her eyes before elbowing him. He sheepishly shrugged. "Okay, we just had lunch, but I always have room for dessert."

After Craig headed outside to take a look at Gracie's yard, the friends sat at the kitchen table, laughing and talking.

"I can't believe my wedding is only weeks away. Some people think I'm nuts for getting married so close to Christmas, but it's what I've dreamed of for years." Kira's eyes held a dreamy gaze.

"I think it's wonderfully romantic, and besides, it's your wedding, so you can marry whenever you'd like." Gracie stood to get the coffee cups, cream, and sugar. "And I'm tickled with my beautiful maid of honor gown. That shade of green will be gorgeous with the red flowers we're carrying." She was honored to be an important part of her friend's wedding ceremony, along with Kira's cousins and future sister-in-law.

"Don't tell the others, but you'll be the prettiest bridesmaid of all, Gracie. Your auburn hair with the dark green dress will be beautiful." Kira reached into her handbag and pulled out several travel brochures. At that moment Craig entered the front door.

"Gracie, can you step into the yard a minute? I want to ask you about the shrubs out front."

Kira remained at the kitchen table while Gracie

accompanied Craig into her yard.

"Okay, this is what I had in mind." He gestured to the small shrubs skirting the front of her house, then explained his ideas for enhancing her landscape, adding color to her small yard.

"Yes, I love your suggestions. That sounds great. Just let me know what I'll owe you."

Craig put a finger to his chin as if in deep thought. "I guess around a million should do it." His serious demeanor lasted only a few seconds.

Gracie punched him in the arm. Before she could toss back her own teasing reply, a voice called to her.

"Hey Miss Gracie! Me and Max is helping Daddy carry groceries in!" Trixie waved as she, Max, and Blake headed toward Blake's car in the driveway.

"Hi Trixie and Max. I'm sure you're very good helpers. Enjoy this pretty weather today." She grinned at them, making only brief eye contact with their father.

Returning her attention to Craig, Gracie complimented his landscaping ideas again. "But you'll need to work on your prices. I'm afraid you'll lose customers with fees like that." They both laughed.

Before Gracie went inside, Craig told her the only charge would be for the price of the flowers he'd plant. When she insisted on paying him for labor, he offered a response that caused her eyes to mist.

"You're Kira's best friend, and you'll be a

big part of our wedding. Consider my work in your yard a little gift. Besides, you're feeding us brownies and pie today." What a great guy her best friend was marrying.

Kira was looking out the kitchen window when she entered, a mischievous grin on her face. She arched an eyebrow in Gracie's direction.

"Your neighbor is one handsome man. And his children are adorable. Didn't you tell me he's widowed?" Kira shot a questioning gaze at her.

"Yes, which is so sad for those little children. To be so young and not have a mother just breaks my heart for them. And they're so sweet and cute. When I spent time with them at the fall festival last weekend, I had as much fun as they did." Gracie felt that now-familiar tug at her heart whenever she saw or thought about Max and Trixie. Glancing out the window, she saw the twins and Blake playing with Pedro.

Kira took her seat at the kitchen table and reached for a brownie. "I have a feeling they really like you. I heard the little girl call to you and wave." Before biting into her brownie, she pinned Gracie with another questioning gaze. "Are you feeling more comfortable around their father? I know you've commented that he doesn't seem very friendly." Kira popped a fudgy bite into her mouth.

Gracie shrugged. "Not really. I've only spoken with him a few times when I've seen them on the beach and then at the fall festival. Trixie is much more outgoing than her dad, and little Max is pretty quiet, so maybe he takes after the dad." She had a feeling about where her friend was headed with this conversation. Sure enough, she was right.

"Well, living next door means you'll have more opportunities to get to know the dad. He sure is handsome. I can't imagine being single and living so close to such a gorgeous hunk." Kira reached for another brownie.

Gracie nibbled at her own brownie, hoping the topic would change. If she revealed to Kira how often she actually thought about Blake, no telling what her well-meaning friend would suggest. Ever since Kira had become engaged, she felt an obligation to help locate someone for her friend, even though Gracie had assured her she was fine with her single status. *For the time being.*

Deliberately switching the conversation to the wedding, Gracie knew she'd have to be careful about mentioning her neighbors. Even an innocent comment about the twins would give Kira an open door to mention Blake, and there was no need to dwell on him. The man was obviously seeing someone, or he was still a grieving widower, although he didn't strike her as being someone in grief.

When Craig came inside, the conversation moved to suggestions for Gracie's yard. After they left, Gracie busied herself doing laundry and re-organizing a shelf. Yet she couldn't shake the unusual feeling deep inside. Almost a feeling of emptiness. What was wrong with her?

She chalked it up to being with the happy couple, so cute as they interacted and teased each other. Gracie was genuinely happy for Kira and honored to be part of their wedding, but it dawned on her she was missing something—a deep yearning in her heart. A yearning for a relationship of her own—and a family someday. Now that she resided in a quaint beach town, would that ever happen? From what she'd observed, this small community didn't have an abundance of single men.

Her eyes landed on a small plaque Aunt Bonnie had given her the year before. The plaque held the last part of a Bible verse from the book of Mark. *All things are possible to him that believeth.*

Gracie was a believer and knew God could do anything. But in her situation, was it likely she'd ever find romance? Thanks to her soured relationship with Derek, she was wary of trusting most men.

She picked up the plaque and ran her fingers over the words. Feeling something soft against her leg, she glanced down. Tubby stretched, then nuzzled his head against her. Gracie smiled and returned the plaque to the kitchen counter, then leaned down to pet her cat's soothing fur. As the words from the Scripture replayed in her mind, peace filled her.

"Okay, I'll just keep praying and keep my eyes open. If the Lord brings my Prince Charming along, I'll be ready." She giggled as the feline gazed up at her with adoration in his green eyes. Gracie didn't have too many specifications about her Prince Charming, but one thing was certain. He *must* like cats.

~ ~ ~

Chapter 5

Blake's boss phoned him Monday regarding the upcoming trip. Even though he was more than a little ready to pursue a new career, he had to meet his current obligations before leaving. The main one being his business trip to South Carolina in December.

"I know you don't like being away from your children, Blake, and this meeting won't require a lengthy stay. You'll fly up on a Friday, attend the training sessions, and fly back on Saturday afternoon. Will you be able to arrange childcare for one night?"

"Yes, I can manage that. I've been reading through the information you e-mailed me and things look pretty clear-cut, so the trip should go smoothly." He forced a positive tone in his words, because his heart certainly wasn't in this.

Given the fact he planned to quit this job, there was no way he could generate any enthusiasm for training in this field. But he couldn't let his boss know his plans until he had things firmly in place. And at the moment he wasn't even close.

"Good, good. We can always count on you. And Blake, no worries on the situation with Chantelle Dawson. I had a conversation with the manager at our Orlando office, and it seems Miss Dawson had been stirring things up there, too. Her manager told me—confidentially, so please don't share this with anyone—that Miss Dawson is under a type of probationary period. If she continues causing conflicts in her local office, she'll be released from the company. The only reason I'm even sharing this with you is because I know her fabricated accusations troubled you, and rightly so. But please put it all behind you, and know that nothing is on your record, because I have no doubt that your character and integrity are of the highest standard."

Wow. Blake had never heard Mr. Whitley speak so highly of him or anyone else in the company, and he was genuinely complimented. Which only made him feel guilty knowing he planned to leave the company within the next six months. Or sooner, if possible.

"Thank you for your words—they mean a lot. And I'm relieved that nothing is on my record since I didn't do anything wrong. But it's a shame that Miss Dawson feels the need to falsely accuse and stir up conflict." Now he was especially thankful he'd declined her invitations to go out—that would've been a huge mistake.

Blake and his boss talked a few more minutes and the call ended. Although he still felt a weight off his shoulders at knowing his record wasn't tarnished, he also couldn't shake the guilt that poked at him. His boss assumed he'd remain with the pharmaceutical company until he retired. Yet he knew that aside from his discontent with his present career, another type of work would allow him more time with his children, and that was his top priority. Yes, if he could make the career change and have more time with the twins, his life would be much better. *But you'll still be single. The twins will be grown someday. You'll be alone.* The silent reminders surfaced in his thoughts and he began thinking of his neighbor.

If Gracie had a romantic interest in her life, then he must live elsewhere and she must hardly ever see him. Blake had been more than a little relieved when he'd learned the male he'd seen recently in Gracie's yard was her friend's fiancé. He'd asked himself again why he cared, but he couldn't deny his attraction to her. Not to mention the fact his children adored her. Should he take a chance and get to know her better? The worst that could happen would be to learn she already had a beau.

If he was ever going to make any changes in his life, he had to get moving. Relocating to Coastal Breeze had been a big step, and he and the twins were happy here. But since he'd made the decision to make a career change, he may as well venture back into the dating scene—at least a little. Surely asking his neighbor out couldn't result in the disasters his previous dates had been, could it? He inwardly cringed as he thought about his former coworkers' attempts at arranging dates. Although his friends meant well, those dates had been big mistakes.

Okay, he'd do it. The next opportunity he had to speak with Gracie he'd find a way to ask her on a date. Maybe including his children would be the best way. Because even though he had no clue how Gracie felt about him, he was certain she was crazy about his kids.

~ ~ ~

The animal clinic was hectic on the days leading up to Thanksgiving, with more people bringing in their dogs for boarding while they traveled. Gracie always felt sad for the animals being left at the clinic, but Dr. Tatum and the other staff stopped in to tend to the animals and always gave them extra attention, according to what the receptionist had told her. At least the animals were safe, and when their owners returned for them, it was a joyful reunion.

"Gracie, what are your Thanksgiving plans?" Dora reached for a handful of candy corn from the festive turkey-shaped dish on the counter.

"I'm going to join Aunt Bonnie and Uncle Fred up in Georgia, and I'm really looking forward to seeing them again. Some other relatives will also be there, so it'll be nice. I'm cooking a few dishes to take so my aunt doesn't have so much to do."

"From the way you've talked about them in the past, I can tell your aunt and uncle are special to you."

"Yes, they've been like parents to me since I lost mine." She forced a smile as she questioned the receptionist about her plans.

"I'll cook and my grown kids will eat with us. Always a good time, even though it'll be more fun when I have grandkids." She winked at Gracie, then arched an eyebrow. "So, you're not taking a special someone with you to the dinner?"

Gracie didn't want the well-meaning receptionist to begin questioning her about Blake, so she shook her head and reached for the next client's folder. Thankfully, the phone rang so Dora was occupied.

She knew Dora had good intentions, but her question only served as a reminder there was no special someone in her life. At least the annoying calls from Derek had ceased, so that was a blessing.

Gracie entered an exam room to administer an oral dewormer to a client's dog. The client had been in before, and he chatted with Gracie about the upcoming holidays.

She opened the vial of yellow medicine and giggled. "This medicine always smells like cupcakes to me." Gracie remembered a recipe she'd recently noticed in a magazine. It gave directions for creating cupcakes that looked like cute Thanksgiving turkeys. She decided to make them for the twins.

Later that day at home, Gracie located the magazine and reviewed the recipe to see exactly what she'd need. A surge of excitement ran through her, which was surprising after the busy day she'd had at the clinic. Too tired to head to the store now, she'd go directly after work tomorrow, then come home and prepare the cupcakes. She couldn't wait to make them for Max and Trixie, and only hoped the cupcakes turned out similar to the magazine photos.

The next day was even busier at the clinic, but Gracie sipped coffee in the breakroom between appointments and the caffeine kept her going. That afternoon she wished her coworkers a happy Thanksgiving and hurried out to her car. She could hardly wait to finish at the grocery store and get home to bake the cupcakes. Pushing her shopping cart briskly up and down the aisles, she grabbed any extra items she thought Aunt Bonnie might need for their dinner, in addition to the ingredients for the cupcakes. As she headed to the checkout line, a voice called to her.

"Miss Gracie!" Trixie ran to her, arms outstretched. Max trotted along behind her grinning shyly. Blake pushed a shopping cart and smiled at her.

"Well hello there, my neighbors." She returned Trixie's hug, tousled Max's dark hair, and grinned at Blake. How handsome he looked in a burgundy shirt that brought out his dark eyes. She also didn't miss the lingering smile he was giving her.

"We're picking up some things for

Thanksgiving dinner at my sister Brianna's in Pensacola. We'll head out Thursday morning and return on Friday. The twins are excited about seeing their grandmother again, since she lives in Arizona now."

"That sounds great. I'll be driving up to Marietta, Georgia, to have dinner with some relatives there, and plan to return Friday. I don't like to leave my cats too long, although they're pretty self-sufficient for a few days." She laughed, then noticed the twins eyeing the contents of her shopping cart. She wanted to keep the cupcakes a surprise, so she wished them a happy Thanksgiving and headed to the checkout line.

"I like Miss Gracie." The sweet voice drifting to her ears tugged at her heart—yet again. But she didn't dare turn around to hear Blake's response to her comment. Maybe he was finally going to act friendlier toward her, because he'd given her a wide smile. Or maybe he was moody, and his moods showed on his face. *Like Derek.* Gracie almost shuddered at the reminder of her ex-boyfriend. No way would she ever have a relationship with someone whose moods fluctuated to that extreme. She'd learned her lesson, and she was much better off single than enduring that pain again.

~ ~ ~

"Don't spill those French fries, Max." They

climbed into the car at the fast-food parking lot. After finishing at the store, Blake decided to treat the twins by picking up burger meals for their supper. He was always amused at how simple activities and treats seemed to thrill his children.

After they'd seen Gracie, Blake had trouble keeping his mind on the items he needed in the store. The fact that Trixie continued mentioning their pretty neighbor didn't help his thoughts stay focused either. He hoped he'd remembered everything, because shopping for groceries wasn't at the top of his fun-things-to-do list.

Pulling into the driveway, he noticed Gracie's car. Since she'd had on her uniform, she must've come there straight from her job at the animal clinic. *She's good with children and animals. And she's beautiful.* So why was she single?

"Since your preschool is closed tomorrow, you can stay up a little later tonight." Blake was glad he'd planned to work from home the next day, because he had a feeling traffic would be heavy with people heading out of town before Thursday.

"Yay!" Max and Trixie chorused.

As his children built with their wooden blocks, Blake tidied up the kitchen and realized he was again thinking about his neighbor. Even after putting in a full day of working with animals, Gracie still looked attractive.

A tapping at the front door pulled him from his thoughts and Trixie called to him. "Daddy, someone's at the door."

Hurrying into the living room, he opened the door to see the woman he'd been thinking about seconds earlier. Gracie was smiling as she held a large plastic container covered with a lid.

Stepping back to invite her inside, Blake stared at the container in her hands. The children hopped up from their blocks and greeted her.

"I thought you might like some turkey cupcakes. They're cupcakes decorated to look like funny turkeys."

Max and Trixie both stood on tiptoe to peek into the container, but the lid concealed the contents.

"May I set these on the table?" She glanced hesitantly at Blake.

"Sure, I should've already suggested that." Luckily, he'd cleaned off the table after their fast-food meal.

When Gracie lifted the plastic lid to reveal a plate filled with colorful, cute cupcakes, both children squealed in delight. Blake was impressed. She must've gone to some trouble to create the little goodies on the plate.

"Are these for us?" Trixie asked, wide-eyed.

"They are, but make sure and check with your dad before you have one. They're very sweet." She glanced up at Blake.

Max licked his lips in anticipation, so Blake told the twins to wash their hands and take a seat at the table.

Blake turned to Gracie to thank her. "This was kind of you. I guess you can tell my kids are thrilled." He offered a wry chuckle, trying to ignore his attraction to the woman standing a mere two feet away.

A light blush colored her face and she nodded. "I'm glad they like the cupcakes. I enjoy doing things for children. When I lived in Georgia, I fixed little treats for my cousin's children. I've missed that since living here, so I'm glad to have your twins living close by."

Was it Blake's imagination or did the blush on her face deepen?

"I guess I'd better go. I've still got a lot to do before driving to see my relatives on Thursday." She headed to the door just as the twins ran toward her, Trixie giving a hug with Max following suit, although a bit timidly.

"Enjoy the turkeys and have a happy Thanksgiving." She grinned at the twins and offered Blake a quick wave, then hurried out the door.

A hint of a floral scent from her perfume lingered after she left. Not heavy, but fresh and appealing. *Like the woman.*

As the children enjoyed a cupcake, Blake thought about their fondness for Gracie. Not only because she brought them treats, but the genuine attention she gave the children showed she sincerely cared about them.

Was it possible she could ever care about him? Maybe after Thanksgiving he'd get to know her better and ask her out. He only hoped things wouldn't turn awkward if she turned him down. Maybe doing activities with the children would be less awkward, and then if the couple hit it off, they could go on actual dates.

To Blake's surprise, the thought gave him a lift,

and when his daughter asked him why he was smiling, he had to fumble with a reply about the cute turkey cupcakes. Trixie accepted his reply, and he had no doubt that his children would accept Miss Gracie if she and their dad were dating.

~ ~ ~

The Saturday after Thanksgiving was windy but sunny as Gracie headed to the beach for an afternoon walk. To her relief there weren't many people out, and she figured some folks were likely shopping. Taking part in the big after-Thanksgiving sales had never appealed to her, especially with online shopping available now.

As she lifted her face to the gulf breeze and heard the squawk of gulls overhead, she thought about the fun family gathering at Aunt Bonnie's. With lots of laughter and good food, the only awkward moment was when one of her cousins asked if she had a 'steady fella,' as the woman phrased it. Gracie had laughed and replied she was happy to be between beaus at the moment.

Now she replayed her response and wondered if she'd been convincing. Because the truth was she was feeling that time was passing her by. Almost thirty years old, still single, with no prospects in sight. Her best friend Kira had already joked about making certain that Gracie caught the bridal bouquet when it was tossed after Kira's wedding.

Shifting her gaze from the blue-green water

to the beach, Gracie saw an approaching couple, strolling and holding hands. The woman was pregnant and as they drew near, the couple's identity became clear. Thomas and Emma Wilton. Emma was the niece of Ginny, the owner of the gift shop in Coastal Breeze.

"Hello there." Emma called to her and Thomas nodded politely.

"Hi, Emma. Hi, Thomas. How are you feeling, Emma?"

"Fat." She burst out laughing as her husband shook his head. "But we're so excited about welcoming our little one in December." She lovingly placed a hand on her rounded belly.

"You don't have much longer to wait, and you don't look fat. You look beautiful." Gracie was sincere, because Emma glowed with the radiance of a woman expecting a precious gift from the Lord.

Emma offered a sweet smile and thanked Gracie for her kind comment. A gust of wind blew past the group so they continued on their way. But Gracie turned and called out. "I'll be eager to hear when the baby arrives."

"I'm sure Aunt Ginny will let everyone know." Emma's words carried on the wind.

As she let the surf glide over her feet, Gracie thought about the cute couple and how happy they seemed. *That's what I want. But it doesn't look likely—at least not living in a small community.*

Not wanting a melancholy mood to ruin her walk, she headed back to her cottage. She'd do some baking when she got home—that always gave her spirit a boost.

As she approached the area where she'd begun her walk, the sound of a small aircraft to her right drew her gaze to the sky above the water. A small plane—apparently from the Air Force base located not too far away—flew over the water. A shudder ran through her, and she quickened her steps.

Maybe she was overreacting. Those men flying military planes were highly trained and skilled, and that was an important part of their work. Yet for Gracie the sight of *any* aircraft— small or large—was only a reminder of her dear parents and the tragic plane crash that had ended their lives. And would've ended her life too if she'd gone with them as originally planned. She fought the tears that formed in her eyes, swiping at them with the back of her hand. The wind whipped her hair and lifted it from her shoulders. Why hadn't she pulled it into a ponytail? The ocean mist mingled with the tears and her eyes stung. She needed to go home.

"Miss Gracie!" Trixie's voice reached her ears and she looked up to see the twins eagerly bounding toward her. As usual, Blake followed with Pedro on a leash.

As she greeted the children, Trixie frowned up at her. "Are you crying?"

There was no way she'd let these precious children know the reason for her tears, so she forced a light laugh and offered an explanation about the ocean mist burning her eyes. Well, it did, so that was truthful.

Blake and Pedro joined them, and to

Gracie's surprise, her handsome neighbor greeted her and asked about her Thanksgiving. Usually it was a polite nod or a limited greeting.

"It was wonderful, thanks for asking. I spent time with relatives I don't see often, and of course we had tons of food. How about you all? Did you enjoy a fun time?"

Blake began to reply when Trixie piped up in an excited voice. "Aunt Brianna is having a wedding! And me and Max get to be in her wedding. I drop flowers and Max is the pillow boy."

Gracie suppressed a laugh at Trixie's descriptions, not wanting to hurt the child's feelings. "How nice. I'm sure you and Max will do a wonderful job in your aunt's wedding." She nibbled her bottom lip and looked up at Blake, who was obviously amused and shaking his head.

"Trixie will be the flower girl and Max will be the ring bearer. My sister Brianna had explained to the children what they'd be doing, and Trixie was amazed at the idea of her brother holding a small pillow in the wedding."

"That's what I figured from her description. I'm sure they'll both be adorable. And congratulations to your sister. When is her wedding?"

"Next spring—mostly likely in May. So there should be plenty of time for the kids to practice their duties for the ceremony."

A plane's engine sounded in the distance, indicating another military aircraft flying along the coast. The twins hopped up and down in excitement at seeing the small plane, and Trixie pointed upward while squealing. "Look, Miss Gracie!"

Gracie's stomach tightened at the sight, but she managed a smile. Time to leave. Right now.

"I'd better return home. Enjoy your walk." She waved at her three neighbors, patted Pedro on the head, and rushed to her car in the small parking area adjacent to the beach. Even though the drive from her cottage to the parking area where she began her walks took all of two minutes, she preferred having her car handy in case bad weather made an unexpected appearance, which happened frequently on the coast. As she drove, her tension eased. Hopefully, Blake didn't notice her hasty departure on the beach, but if he did, there was nothing she could do about it.

Once home from her walk, Gracie decided to bake cookies. As she gathered the ingredients and preheated the oven, she thought about Trixie's announcement of her aunt's wedding. She couldn't help wondering if Blake would also take part in the ceremony—perhaps be a groomsman.

How handsome he would be in a nice suit or a tux. Of course, the man was handsome even dressed casually, as he'd been today on the beach. When the wind had tousled his dark hair and he'd turned to gaze out at the water, he'd looked so attractive. In a refined sort of way. He wasn't the muscular, gym-workout kind of guy, although he appeared to be in good shape and took care of himself. But he definitely looked the part of a businessman, and the few times he broke out in a wide grin, it did something to her heart. *You need to rein in those feelings, because he's shown absolutely zero interest in you—except as a casual neighbor.* She sighed.

As she finished baking the sugar cookies and mixed up the icing to decorate them, she heard the engine of another small plane. Purposely avoiding her window, Gracie suppressed a shudder and stirred the bowl of icing with a vengeance. She needed to overcome her reaction to those planes, especially now that she lived not far from an Air Force base. A stab of guilt nudged her as she realized she had not been praying about her fear as she should. Come to think of it, she'd not been praying about anything as she should—including her future.

Applying colorful icing to the cookies, Gracie made up her mind that she'd be more deliberate in her prayer time. Prayer was powerful, and if she wanted guidance about her future life and present fears, she couldn't do it in her own power.

~ ~ ~

December arrived with cooler temperatures, and Gracie tugged her jacket tightly around her as she hurried inside her house. The days were definitely getting shorter, and darkness came much earlier now.

After feeding her cats and changing clothes, she put a frozen chicken pie in her oven to bake, then decided to go through some Christmas ornaments. Lifting a large plastic tub from her guest bedroom closet, she opened it to find a box of assorted Christmas figurines her mother had kept over the years. Refusing to allow sad feelings to creep in at the reminder of her parents, she snapped the lid on the tub and retrieved another Christmas tub. This one contained figurines and ornaments that Gracie had accumulated, yet she realized some of them had collected dust. Might as well step outside to dust them rather than have dust floating around inside her home. She grabbed a dust cloth, a box of decorations, and stepped out her back door. If she remained outside more than a few minutes she'd need her jacket, but she planned to accomplish this quickly.

"Miss Gracie, what'cha doing?" Trixie called to her as she and Max, followed by Pedro, ran to the fence. Their little faces peering through the chain-links made a precious sight, and Gracie felt that now-familiar tug at her heart.

She was about to reply, then decided she'd go to the fence and show them. Careful not to drop the box of figurines, she set it in the grass near the fence, then lifted out a few so the twins could see them. "I want to set them out in my house before Christmas, but they needed to be dusted. I came outside so the dust wouldn't be inside my house. I don't want my kitties to start sneezing." She added her last statement with a wink and the twins giggled. At that moment Blake called them.

"Time to eat supper, kids." He ambled over

toward his children, who remained at the fence. As he drew closer, his gaze met Gracie's and he offered a grin and casual greeting before tousling Max's hair.

Trixie turned to her father. "Daddy, look what Miss Gracie has. Christmas things."

"Those are very nice."

She quickly explained she'd brought the small box of figurines outside for dusting, and when the twins had noticed them, she'd brought them to the fence so they could have a closer look.

"That was nice of Miss Gracie to show you her pretty decorations. But now it's time for you both to head inside and wash your hands to eat supper."

Was it her imagination, or were the twins hesitant to leave the fence? Most likely they enjoyed playing outside rather than reluctance to leave her company. Trixie's next words were totally unexpected.

"Daddy, you said we're gonna get a Christmas tree soon, so can Miss Gracie come with us?" The child gazed innocently up at her father, who was also caught off guard at her question.

"Well, uh...that would be fine, but I'm sure Miss Gracie has her own tree to take care of." He stuffed his hands in his pockets, clearly uncomfortable.

"Do you, Miss Gracie? You could still help us pick out our tree." Trixie's gaze bounced between her father and Gracie like a tennis ball. Max remained quiet and was petting Pedro, but a few times glanced up as if not wanting to miss anything.

"Thank you for thinking of me, Trixie. Yes, I do

need to get my Christmas tree soon, and I know you and Max will enjoy picking out your tree with your dad." Gracie spoke cheerfully, hoping this conversation would end and she'd head back inside. But she wasn't prepared for the crestfallen expression on Trixie's face. She looked like she was going to cry.

"See? Miss Gracie needs to get her own tree. Now let's go have our supper. Tell Miss Gracie you'll see her another time." Blake shot her a sympathetic grin, as if letting her know he understood she'd been put on the spot just as he had.

"Good-bye, Trixie and Max. I'll see you again before long." She smiled sweetly at the children, still bothered that Trixie appeared disappointed. Grasping the box of figurines, Gracie all but ran to her back door and scooted inside.

But once in her kitchen, she couldn't resist a peek out her window as Blake ushered his children into their house. Even in the dusk, the slump of Trixie's small shoulders tugged at her heart. She could tell that Blake was a concerned, loving father to the twins, and it was good that he planned to take them to get a Christmas tree soon. That would be a fun family activity for them. *And you wish you were joining them.* The unexpected thought jolted her, and she almost dropped the small ceramic Christmas tree.

Yet Gracie knew it would likely be awkward if she joined them in an activity, because she wasn't part of their family. That would require a relationship with the twins' father—a *romantic* relationship. And while that thought held appeal to her, she'd only observed a politeness from Blake— nothing even remotely akin to a real interest in her. If she was truthful with herself, that bothered her more than she cared to admit.

~ ~ ~

Oh, he'd really blown it. Inviting Gracie to join them in picking out a Christmas tree might've been the perfect activity to get to know their pretty neighbor. Yet he'd fumbled around and acted as if he didn't want her to join them. He wasn't rude, but he'd cut off his daughter's innocent suggestion. Now he was reminded of his hasty reply as he watched Trixie's melancholy mood at supper.

Even Max noticed his sister's temperament and glanced at his father. "What's wrong with Trixie?" He asked between bites of soup.

Trixie aimed a slight scowl at her brother before redirecting the look toward her father. "Nothin'. But Dad won't let Miss Gracie go with us when we get our tree, and it would be funner with Miss Gracie." She plopped her spoon in the bowl of vegetable soup, sending little splatters onto the placemat.

"Trixie, don't drop your spoon like that. You might spill your soup." Blake then turned to Max. "I wouldn't mind having Miss Gracie join us, but I thought she might be busy. People get very busy near Christmas."

To Blake's surprise, Max offered a shrug and

commented. "You could ask her, dad. Miss Gracie is nice, and she makes good cookies." He resumed eating as if that was all he had to say on the matter.

Okay, he needed to handle this carefully. Trixie shouldn't think that pouting was a tool she could use to get her way. Yet this wasn't a big deal—just going to choose a Christmas tree. Besides, his kids adored their neighbor. Blake released a long sigh and finished his last bite of soup.

"The next time we see Miss Gracie, we can ask her if she'd like to join us when we get our Christmas tree." As Trixie squealed in delight, Blake held up a finger. "But—if she says she cannot go with us, I don't want any complaining. Got it?"

Both children bobbed their heads as they grinned. Then in unison they replied. "Got it."

The next morning Blake drove the twins to preschool, then returned home to prepare for his upcoming trip. With each passing day he became more and more restless to leave his current position and begin a new career. Yet he still had much to do before that could happen, not to mention the glaring fact that he didn't *have* a new career. At least not yet. Right now he must focus on his trip to South Carolina to attend a training session for the pharmaceutical company. He tried to ignore the dull pain in his right side, assuming it was caused by gulping down his breakfast before driving the twins.

Later that day as Blake drove the children

home from preschool, Max asked about the Christmas tree. As usual, his talkative twin joined in. "Yes, Daddy, when can we get our Christmas tree? Miss Katie at our preschool says we'll have one in our classroom soon. But we want one at home, too."

Blake released a sigh, feeling a bit overwhelmed. He needed to finish preparations for his business trip, search for a new career, and most importantly be a good dad to his twins. Right now he didn't feel successful in any of those areas. But he attempted to sound upbeat. "Don't worry, kids. I promise we'll get our Christmas tree very soon." He practically held his breath as he waited for Trixie to ask about their neighbor joining them, but she spied a dog in someone's yard and exclaimed over the animal.

When they arrived home, he gave the twins a snack and put on a children's movie, then resumed his work at the table. The ring of the phone broke his concentration. Brianna's perky voice came through.

"Hi big brother. Just checking to see if your trip to South Carolina is still on. We need to finalize details about childcare." What would Blake do without his sister? He had no clue.

"Thanks, Bri. I'm glad you phoned because I'd planned to touch base with you later today. Yeah, unfortunately the trip is still on. I fly up there Friday morning and return home Saturday afternoon. Are you certain my trip won't interfere with your college finals or anything else? Because if it does, then I'll make other arrangements." What was he saying? He didn't *have* any other arrangements he could make for his children. His mother and Sarge and Nora lived too far away to lend a helping hand.

"No, this actually works out well, because my finals are the following Monday and Tuesday, so I'll just be studying on the days I need to help with the kiddos. I'm happy to help. Those twins are a good distraction, and after this semester at college, I need a distraction." The sound of her laughter offered a bit of soothing reassurance to Blake's frazzled mood.

"Thanks, Bri. I don't know what I'd do without you."

She giggled. "Too bad you didn't feel this way when we were growing up."

After a few more minutes of discussing the classes Brianna had taken and the upcoming Christmas holidays, their call ended. Blake grabbed a cola from the refrigerator and got back to work. At least knowing his children would be well-cared-for while he was traveling gave him peace of mind, so he could focus on his travel preparations and then peruse more information on a new career. Which so far hadn't offered many leads. A quick glance into the living room let him know the children were engrossed in the movie.

Shortly before Blake stopped working to prepare supper, Trixie exclaimed. "I heard Miss Gracie's car. Can we go ask her to get a Christmas tree with us?" Even Max's attention was diverted from the movie as he ran to the window to peer out beside his sister.

Might as well do this. "Get your jackets and we'll go to Miss Gracie's door. But we're not going for a visit, so don't ask to see her cats or stay and visit a while. Besides, it's almost suppertime." He assisted the twins with their jackets before the trio headed to Gracie's house.

A festive evergreen wreath adorned with a lovely bow and some small jingle bells hung from the door. From inside her house Christmas music drifted out to their ears. It was obvious she loved Christmas. He tapped on the door.

Genuine surprise covered her face when she opened the door. "Hello there. Would you like to come in? I know it's a little breezy today."

Blake was prepared to place his hands on the twins' shoulders if necessary to keep them on the porch with him. He shook his head and explained their reason for coming to her door. "My children can be quite persistent, so I told them we'd ask if you would care to join us when we go to get our tree. Actually, I'm not even sure when we'll go, because I have an out-of-town trip this Friday." He hesitated, aggravated with himself for not thinking this through beforehand. Might as well forge ahead. "How about tomorrow after you get home from work? If that's not good, we'll try another time. Um…assuming you'd like to join us, of course." He was rambling. A businessman who'd met with numerous doctors and medical professionals, and here he sounded like a fool with his neighbor.

Gracie gazed at his twins with a playful gleam in her eyes. "Hmmm…this sounds like a fun adventure, and I can't pass up an adventure." Trixie and Max giggled, then Trixie hopped up and down.

"Does this mean you're gonna go with us, Miss Gracie?"

"Yes, Trixie. I'd love to go with you to choose your Christmas tree. But I have a big favor to ask your dad." She looked shyly up at Blake. "Would you mind terribly if I also got my tree at the same time? Would there be room on the roof of your car for two trees? Mine would be small." She nibbled her bottom lip, as if apprehensive.

"Sure, that's fine. My SUV should be able to manage two trees, and that would save you a trip." He only hoped *he* could manage getting both trees tied down to his vehicle's roof without losing one on their drive home.

They told Gracie good-bye and headed to their door, but when Blake glanced back as they crossed his driveway, she was still standing in her doorway, smiling and waving. To his surprise it wasn't only his children who were looking forward to the Christmas tree outing with their neighbor. Who knows—maybe this was an opportunity to get to know her better.

~ ~ ~

PATTI JO MOORE

Chapter 6

"Mmm, there's nothing like the fragrance of fir trees at Christmas." Gracie sniffed at several evergreens as she, Blake, and the twins meandered through the Christmas tree lot the next afternoon. Darkness was fast approaching and the colorful lights strung around the area added a cozy glow to the cool evening.

"Look at this one, Miss Gracie." Max tugged at her hand to show her a large tree he'd discovered, while Trixie bounced in excitement as she darted from one tree to the next. Although Gracie always loved this wonderful time of year, being with these sweet children added something more special to the season. Such wonder and innocence lit up their little faces, which endeared them even more to her heart. She knew it was silly, but for a few minutes, she pretended that the twins were *her* children and they were on a family outing. *What about Blake?* Dare she imagine how it would be if they really were a family? An unexpected tingle ran through her at the thought of being married to Blake. His voice jolted her from the ridiculous daydream, and she knew a blush covered her face.

"Have you found your tree yet?" He stood close and his musky cologne reached her nose. Combined with the fir trees, the scent was a pleasing mixture of fragrances. He eyed her curiously.

"Uh, not yet. But I will soon. I've just been admiring all the trees. Kind of like a kid in a candy store." She giggled and gave herself a mental shake. No more daydreaming while she was here. Besides, she needed to find her own tree.

Blake pulled a tree away from the others so the twins could have a better view. "What do you think? This one is nice and tall, but not too big. We don't need a big tree in our living room." The twins circled the tree, as if inspecting the branches. Max nodded, and Trixie gave her approval.

"Good. I'll let a worker know this is the one we're getting." Blake lugged the tree to a nearby middle-aged man in a ballcap, who quickly assisted him with the fir.

"Did you find a tree, Miss Gracie?" A slight frown appeared on Trixie's face as she grasped Gracie's right hand.

"Not yet, but I will. Could you and Max help me? I don't need a big tree, but maybe something about this tall." She used her free hand to show the twins the height she'd like.

Both Trixie and Max appeared to take the task seriously as they examined trees and sniffed the branches. Several times they pointed to one and asked if she liked it. Finally, Max pointed to one that Gracie thought would be ideal for her living room.

"Yes! I think this one is just the right size. Thank you, Max. And thank you, Trixie, for all your help. I have a feeling that Tubby and Cheddar will like this tree too." At the mention of her cats, both twins laughed. Blake approached them with his wallet in one hand, a grin on his handsome face.

"Daddy, we helped Miss Gracie find a tree!" Trixie announced proudly.

"Good job, kids. Gracie, I've got my wallet out if you'll let me pay for your tree."

This was totally unexpected, and although very kind and generous, there was no way she would agree to his offer. She smiled while shaking her head. "You are so nice to offer, but I insist on paying for my own tree. I appreciate you allowing me to join you and for these kiddos' help."

He shrugged and took the tree from her grasp, their hands touching briefly. The tingle returned and coursed through her, and her earlier daydream of being part of this family threatened to return, but she shoved it away. Lifting her wallet from her handbag, Gracie scooted to the small table set up for tree payments.

The man with the ballcap who'd assisted Blake now took her money and gave her an amused grin. "So your family is gettin' two trees, huh? Now that's nice. I imagine your kids get real excited at Christmas time." He counted out her change. "Yep, my wife and I miss those days when the kids were little, like your kids are now. You enjoy every minute, because afore you know it, those young'uns will be grown and moved away." The man's well-meaning comments were only heard by Gracie, to her relief. Blake and the twins were at his car where a young man hoisted both trees to the vehicle roof.

Gracie thanked the man, then wished him a merry Christmas and joined Blake and the twins. He grinned at her and held up a roll of twine.

"It's a good thing I brought my own, because this fellow says they're almost out." He stepped over to assist with the tying.

After climbing into the car for the return drive home, Blake nodded his head as he drove out of the small parking lot. "I'll have to remember this place for next year. Those guys were nice and the trees all seemed fresh."

Hearing her dad's comment, Trixie asked. "Can you come with us next year to get a Christmas tree, Miss Gracie? This was fun."

Glancing over toward Blake, Gracie tried to think of a reply, but Blake spoke first. "Next year is a long way off. Let's enjoy this Christmas." His comments were followed by a grin aimed at Gracie. His grin sent a tingle rushing through her, but she told herself it was the chill in the evening air.

Gracie asked if they enjoyed decorating their tree each Christmas. By the time Blake reached her driveway, she was giggling at Trixie's enthusiastic replies about her favorite ornaments and the ones they were making at preschool. Max chimed in with a description of his favorite reindeer ornament. Nothing like a child's excitement at Christmas to boost everyone's spirits.

Blake instructed the children to remain in the car as he untied Gracie's tree and carried it to her front door. "Do you need help putting it in the tree stand? I know that can be a hassle sometimes." His nearness sent a wave of warmth rushing through her.

For a moment she had the impulse to blurt out yes, but she caught herself and explained her friend, Kira, and her fiancé, Craig, were planning to help her set it up. "But if it's okay with you, I'd love for Max and Trixie to help me with the decorating later on."

As their gazes met, there was a flicker of something in Blake's eyes—appreciation?—and a smile spread across his face. "Sure, they would love that. I'll be gone overnight on a business trip this Friday, and my sister Brianna will be staying with them. But if you invite them over, I'm sure Bri would be okay with that."

Gracie thanked him again for his help with her tree, waved good-night to the twins, and unlocked her front door. She'd leave the tree on her small porch until her friends arrived the next afternoon to help.

When her cell phone vibrated she remembered she'd cut off the volume while she was with Blake and the twins, so she quickly answered. Aunt Bonnie's worried voice came through and guilt pricked at Gracie for causing her aunt distress. "I'm sorry you phoned several times with no answer. I never want you to worry about me. I went with some neighbors to get my Christmas tree."

"I'm so relieved you weren't out after dark alone, Gracie dear. I'm sure Coastal Breeze is a safe area, but you're an attractive young woman and you must be careful."

Gracie couldn't deny feeling grateful for her aunt's concern. At least she had relatives who cared about her and wanted to make sure she was okay. She thanked Bonnie and promised she'd not leave her volume off again.

Her aunt explained the reason for her original call. "I know we'd talked about having you join us for Christmas dinner, but our long-time friends, Janice and Marty, have invited us to their lovely cabin in the north Georgia mountains. At first, I declined their invitation, but Janice persisted. After Marty's bout with cancer, I'd feel terrible if we didn't spend time with him and he became sick again. So...would you mind terribly if your uncle and I were gone for the Christmas holidays? I just want to make certain you're okay with this, but I don't want you to be alone. Nothing is sadder than a person being alone on a special holiday."

Although Gracie was disappointed, she wanted only the best for her aunt and uncle. If they would enjoy a trip with friends, that's what they should do. And especially since one of their friends had been so ill and was now doing better—all the more reason they should go to the mountains.

"You and Uncle Fred should absolutely go with Janice and Marty. You deserve a trip away, and from what you've told me in the past, their cabin is lovely." Gracie remembered Bonnie's description of the cabin, and it sounded like a wonderful place to spend Christmas. Or any day.

Bonnie's tone was hesitant. "Are you certain, Gracie? The thoughts of you being all alone at Christmas hurt my heart. Now remember you do have your cousins so you could join them for a celebration."

Bless Aunt Bonnie—she had such good intentions. But there was no way Gracie would home in on her cousins' special time with their own families. Forcing an upbeat tone, she replied. "Thank you for suggesting that, but I promise I'll be fine. Now I want you and Uncle Fred to get busy planning that trip to the mountains. And enjoy that lovely stone fireplace you've told me about—it sounds so cozy."

After talking a few more minutes, their call ended. Gracie was genuinely happy for her aunt and uncle having the opportunity to do something out of the ordinary for Christmas. Who knows—maybe one day Gracie would have a special someone to spend Christmas with in a lovely mountain cabin. *Yeah, right. Don't expect that anytime soon.* She ignored the taunting voice in her mind and sorted through a box of Christmas decorations. Yet as she gently handled the angel and snowflake ornaments, her thoughts drifted to earlier that evening at the tree lot with Blake and the twins. What would it be like to spend Christmas with them? The thought made her smile—yet she knew it was only a thought.

Although the kids seemed crazy about her, and their father had even managed a smile, the ice in him still hadn't melted. Romance was a long way off.

~ ~ ~

"Daddy, why are you frowning?" Trixie questioned as Blake made sure he had everything necessary for his brief business trip to South Carolina. The pain in his side had become more frequent and was an annoyance. He needed to focus on the upcoming training sessions without a pesky pain distracting him.

He gently tugged Trixie's ponytail and winked at her. "I'm making sure I haven't forgotten anything I need for my meetings. Now remember that Aunt Brianna will be staying with you while I'm away, and before you and Max know it, I'll be home again."

Trixie nodded in her usual accepting manner before she began babbling about the games Aunt Brianna would play with them. Max came into the room and his tousled hair was a reminder that Blake needed to get his children ready for preschool. He had planned to drop them off before making the drive to the airport. Brianna would pick up the twins at preschool and stay with them until Blake returned home Saturday afternoon. And his return home couldn't come quickly enough. He'd been dreading being away from his children ever since his boss informed him of this trip.

To Blake's relief the children didn't appear sad when he hugged them good-bye at their preschool classroom, and he quietly reminded their teacher of his trip and the childcare arrangements with his sister. Yes, it appeared everything was all worked out and the twins were happy. Once this trip was behind him, he'd breathe again. *If the pain would stop.*

He reached the airport with plenty of time to spare, so he hoped having some downtime in the waiting area would calm his stomach and the pain would subside. Surprisingly, the idea of another cup of coffee made him queasy. Must be nerves, although there was nothing about the meetings to cause him to be nervous.

"Are you saving this seat?" A sultry, smooth female voice interrupted his thoughts.

Blake looked up into the heavily made-up eyes of a woman who appeared to be in her thirties. Her short, black hair and red outfit were stylish and she exuded confidence. Maybe *too much* confidence.

He shook his head. "No, it's available." Poor choice of words on his part. He certainly didn't want this woman to think *he* was available, even though he was. Only one woman kept creeping into his thoughts—a certain auburn-haired neighbor.

The woman slowly lowered her body into

the chair, crossed her toned legs and angled slightly toward him. Blake tensed up, which would not help his stomach pain at all. He hoped she wouldn't begin a conversation, because he didn't feel like talking to anyone, much less her.

To his relief the woman's cell phone rang and she became engrossed in a conversation which lasted until they were called to begin boarding the plane. Now if his pain would ease up, things would be fine—provided the woman wasn't seated beside him on the plane.

The flight was uneventful and Blake maintained a semi-comfortable position in the aisle seat beside an older man who slept the entire time. He only hoped whatever was causing his pain would lessen—or vanish completely.

His cell phone rang as he was getting settled in his hotel room. The first meeting wouldn't begin for forty-five minutes, so he had time to rest before heading downstairs to the conference room. He smiled as Trixie's voice came through, excitedly telling him what she and Max had done at preschool. Brianna soon got on.

"Sorry if we're interrupting, big brother. The twins were so excited about decorating Christmas cookies at preschool today and Trixie was about to burst to tell you."

"It's fine, Bri. I always love hearing my children's voices. Is everything going okay there?"

"Sure, no problems at all. I hope your meetings go smoothly and then you'll have this behind you. I know you're eager to pursue your new career."

"That's an understatement." Blake laughed, not

wanting to tell his sister about his symptoms. "Guess I'd better change clothes before my meeting starts. But I'll keep my phone with me if you need to text while I'm in a meeting. Give the twins a big hug from me."

After he clicked off his phone, he hoped Brianna hadn't detected anything unusual in his tone. He was afraid the pain was causing him to sound tense, and he didn't want his sister or twins to worry. Maybe it was just the spicy pizza he'd eaten last night. Or nerves from the need to tell his boss about his plans to leave the company. He'd do his best to focus on the meetings and ignore his discomfort. Maybe sipping a cola during the first meeting would help.

Blake managed to get through the remainder of Friday with no major issues—only the nagging pain, sometimes worse than other times. He declined an offer to join several men at a steak restaurant, choosing instead to grab a sandwich from the hotel café and eat in his room.

His sleep was fitful that night, and he woke up exhausted in the morning. What was wrong with him? Fear crept in, aggravating the pain in his stomach and his overwhelming fatigue. Well, he couldn't remain in his hotel bed, so he'd have to force himself to shower, get dressed, and head to the morning session.

Another attendee leaned toward him as the men took their seats. "Are you okay? You don't look like you feel well."

Blake shook his head, appreciating the man's concern but not wanting to draw attention to himself. "Nah, I think something I ate is giving me a rough time. No worries, it's not contagious."

The other man nodded and didn't slide his chair away, which Blake had expected him to do. "I'll be okay." Blake added, hoping to convince not only the attendee but also himself.

He managed to survive the morning, counting down the hours until he could board his plane and head back to Florida. Back to his precious twins. *And see my beautiful neighbor again.* Where had that thought come from?

At lunchtime Blake again declined an offer to join others for a meal at a nearby restaurant and refrained from buying anything to eat at the hotel café. Heading to the elevator, his side pain worsened. He needed to reach his room so he could collapse on the hotel bed and rest before leaving for the airport. *You'll be fine. You'll be fine.* He repeated the words over and over, hoping to convince himself. Except the words didn't help. The pain was getting the best of him.

"Blake!" One of the men called to him as he staggered onto the elevator. He reached out his hand to try and grab hold of something, but there was nothing to grab. The walls of the elevator seemed to spin around and around. "Blake!" The voice became louder, the walls spun faster…and everything went black.

~ ~ ~

What an unexpected change in plans, but a welcome one. Gracie opened her front door on Saturday morning to a frantic Brianna, with the twins standing beside her. "Good morning. Would you like to come in?" She stepped back as the trio entered, immediately feeling Trixie's arms around her waist in a hug.

"I am so sorry to drop by like this, but I have a huge favor to ask. A *really* huge favor. My cousin Sami has just gone into labor, and I'd promised to be with her when her baby arrives since her husband is serving in the army and is stationed in the Middle East. The baby isn't due for at least two more weeks, but Sami is in labor now and I need to be with her. Is there any way you can keep the twins until Blake gets home from his South Carolina trip? His plane should land around three o'clock, and then it's just a matter of him driving home from the airport." Brianna paused long enough to catch her breath before continuing. "If you have other plans I understand and I'll try to work out something else. But I know the kiddos don't need to accompany me to the hospital—I'm going straight there—and they talk about you a lot. I can tell you're special to them." The younger woman's eyes were pleading as she spoke, and Trixie was gently squeezing Gracie's left hand, as if to convince her to say yes.

"Of course, they can stay with me. I'd be thrilled to have them and was planning to invite them over anyway to help me with some

Christmas decorating." She grinned at both Trixie and Max, tweaking Max's nose as he giggled.

Brianna's shoulders visibly relaxed. "Thank you so much! You don't know what a tremendous relief this is. I will do something special for you to thank you for helping, and I know Blake will be appreciative too. I tried to text him to let him know what's going on, but he must be in a meeting because he didn't respond. But he's mentioned you, too, so I know this would be agreeable with him." A tiny sparkle glinted in Brianna's eyes as she'd made the comment about her brother mentioning her.

"It's not a problem at all—I promise. And I'll be praying for your cousin and the baby. I sure hope everything will go well."

"Thank you again. Here's a door key in case I've forgotten something they might need. You're an angel." Suddenly Brianna leaned over and gave Gracie a quick hug, then pulled away as if embarrassed.

"I'm happy to help." She smiled, wanting to reassure Blake's sister that she'd not been offended by the hug.

"Okay, kiddos. Now be good for Miss Gracie, and your daddy should be home before long. Thanks again, Gracie. You really are as wonderful as they've said." With that, Brianna was out the door, leaving Gracie wondering who 'they' were. Most likely the twins. But could Blake have possibly said something positive to his sister about her? She'd have to ponder that later, because right now she had plenty to do to ensure the children enjoyed their time at her house. She placed the door key on her kitchen counter, making a mental note so she'd remember.

"Let's see…what to do first." Gracie rubbed her hands together as if plotting a major project. Her heart warmed at the eager faces peering up at her.

"Miss Gracie, can we bake cookies?" Trixie's eyes were wide with anticipation.

"Yeah…cookies!" Max added his agreement.

How could she possibly resist these precious children? After a slight pause as she pretended to be giving the request some serious thought, Gracie pointed toward her kitchen and the twins squealed in delight.

Fifteen minutes later there were giggling children, small piles of flour, and brightly-colored sprinkles in Gracie's kitchen. It was a mess, but she loved every bit of this fun messy time. Even her felines sat in the doorway, surveying the scene in quiet fascination.

She glanced at her stove clock and thought about what Brianna had said earlier. Blake was probably headed to the airport for his flight back to Florida. At the thought of the twins' father boarding a large plane, Gracie's stomach clenched and her pulse quickened. She needed to say a silent prayer for his safe travel and then focus on the excited children in her care.

"Look, Miss Gracie!" Max proudly displayed the Christmas tree-shaped cookie he'd decorated, complete with an abundance of sprinkles.

"Oh, Max...that is a beautiful Christmas tree. It looks good enough to eat."

The children erupted in more giggles, as Trixie explained to her that cookies are meant to be eaten. Gracie played along, pretending she'd forgotten since Max had decorated it so well.

After baking cookies, they headed to the tree. Gracie was glad Kira and her fiancé had set the tree in its stand. There was no way she could've handled that by herself. It had been an enjoyable evening with Kira and Craig, cooking supper for them, and chatting about their upcoming wedding.

"Mmm...your tree smells good, Miss Gracie. It smells like our tree." Trixie gazed at the assortment of ornaments in a box on the coffee table.

"Yes, it does smell good. That's my favorite smell in the world—besides my pot of coffee when it's brewing." Gracie slid the box that Trixie had been eyeing close to her, noting the child's pleased expression. "Trixie, this can be your box of ornaments to hang on the tree, and I've got this box for Max."

Max's eyes lit as he peered into the one before him.

Then Trixie asked in concern. "But Miss Gracie, what are *you* gonna put on the tree?"

Gracie laughed, touched that the young child was thinking about someone other than herself. She winked at Trixie and gestured to another box, lifting off the lid to show the shiny round ornaments inside. "I'll hang these on the tree. It should look beautiful after we all put our boxes of decorations on it."

Five minutes later both twins were busily hanging ornaments as a Christmas music CD played in the background. Even though Gracie was also hanging a few ornaments, she enjoyed observing the children. Even if she wasn't married with children of her own, she was still getting to enjoy doing special Christmas activities with these precious little ones, and for that she was very thankful.

Just as Gracie was pondering what to prepare the twins for lunch, her cell phone rang. She froze as Brianna's panicked voice came through.

"Gracie, I have some bad news. Blake's in the hospital in Greenville. He's being prepped for surgery. He wants the twins with him."

"Oh no, that's terrible. What type of surgery?" She glanced at the children and regretted her words.

"It's his appendix. Serious but not critical."

"What can I do to help? The kids are fine here."

"My car battery died and I'm stuck here at the hospital waiting for Sami to deliver her baby. I know it's a lot to ask, but could you fly with the twins to Greenville? Don't worry about the cost. Blake will take care of everything."

"I...I, of course." Gracie's pulse raced.

"Good. While you get ready, I'll go online and see about your tickets. I know this is a huge thing to ask, but I'm really worried about Blake. If there was any way, I'd take the twins myself. I-I think after losing his wife, Blake is extra-worried about the children. They've lost their mother, and now he wants to assure them he isn't leaving them. I'm so glad I left their house key with you, so you can grab a few things for the twins." Brianna paused to catch her breath before continuing.

"I have power of attorney over Blake's children, so I'll hurry and write a letter giving you permission to accompany them. I'll leave it with the receptionist at the main desk, if you can swing by here on your way to the airport. Remember, Blake will take care of all the expenses, so don't worry."

Paying for the expenses were not what worried her. But Gracie couldn't very well blurt out her fear of flying to Brianna. Gripping the phone so tightly her hand ached, Gracie tried to steady herself as her mind whirled. Surely this was a bad dream.

Blake's sister wasn't really on the phone, telling her she needed to accompany the twins on an airplane flight, was she? No, no, no! There was *no way* Gracie Norton was getting near a plane—much less setting foot on one. Bile rose in her throat and for a few seconds she wondered if she was going to be sick. Right there in her living room in front of the twins. She managed a measured breath, hoping it might calm her. Even though the children were still decorating the tree, they cast curious glances her way.

"Gracie? Are you there? Did all my conversation come through, or did we lose connection for part of it?"

"I-I'm here." That was all she could say at that moment. Brianna had no idea what the thought of flying did to Gracie, and she had no idea that the request she'd made was out of the question. Impossible.

~ ~ ~

PATTI JO MOORE

Chapter 7

What was she doing here? She did not belong in an airport. Especially not with her neighbor's twins in tow. Yet here they were, after taking an Uber from her house to the hospital to get the letter from Brianna, then on to the airport. Gracie somehow managed to usher the kids and a bag through the terminal's entryway.

She could not do this. What if she fainted? The responsibility for two innocent, young children was a major job—she absolutely *had* to stay focused and remain calm for them. But could she do that? Her palms were sweating as she grabbed her bag with one hand and Max's little hand in her other. She'd told Trixie to stay right beside her as they walked. Each step seemed weighted down, as if her legs were telling her to turn around and go home.

Spotting a bench, she told the twins they'd sit for a few minutes. With trembling hands she dug out the tickets she'd printed at home, thankful that Brianna had checked on available flights and phoned her with the information. Earlier she'd been moving in a fog while at Blake's house, grabbing a few clothes and toothbrushes while trying to reassure the twins that this would be an adventure. She didn't tell them their father was ill—not after they'd lost their mother. Thankfully there would only be one bag to check since she'd packed the children's items in her luggage.

"Miss Gracie, this place is noisy." Trixie peered up at her and Gracie forced a smile as she nodded.

"Yes, Trixie. Airports are busy places. Max, please make sure you stay with me so no one gets lost." She stood and the children rose too, hovering close to her side.

"Why didn't Aunt Brianna come with us, too?" Trixie's question caused Gracie to display a temporary calmness she didn't feel—at all.

"Sweetie, Aunt Brianna would've joined us, but she has to stay with Cousin Sami and wait for the baby to be born." Whew. That reply appeared to satisfy Trixie.

Gracie tried to steady her breathing, but her heart pounded and she was again fearful of becoming lightheaded. Once they'd checked in their bag, they headed to security, but as she approached the line, her steps slowed. She couldn't do this. Uninvited memories of her parents' plane crash erupted in her mind. The call she'd received. The photo of the mangled plane. Thoughts of their last moments. It was *too much*.

Her head throbbed and tears threatened. Both

twins gazed curiously up at her. Gracie had come to a standstill, and the children surely must be wondering what was going on. Now Trixie wore a puzzled frown and Max's little face was filled with uncertainty. "Why are we stopping, Miss Gracie?" The child's question was the nudge Gracie needed to put one foot in front of the other.

"I'm just feeling a bit tired, sweetie." She offered a forced smile to both twins and then kept her eyes straight ahead, knowing she had no choice but to continue.

Lord, I cannot do this on my own. If I'm to accompany these precious children to see their father, You will have to help me. Please, Lord. I am desperate. The prayer offered a tiny ray of hope. She knew the Bible verse that said all things were possible with God. Did she truly believe it? She'd always thought she did, but now it was being put to the test.

The security line wasn't long, so Gracie and the twins made it through in only a few minutes. The security agent had studied the children's birth certificates, pored over the letter, then asked the twins a few questions. When he stamped their boarding passes, Gracie finally allowed herself to breathe. The children appeared fascinated with all the sights and sounds, which was good. The hustle and bustle would distract them from noticing her fear. Or asking questions about their father—who was lying in a hospital bed at that moment.

As the trio stepped onto the plane, Gracie

again froze. Her feet were weighted down, as if glued to the floor. Each step took effort. She was actually *on* a plane—something she'd vowed she would never again do. She told herself this was a jet rather than a small private plane as her parents had been on that fateful day. *Don't think about it.* She must not let horrible memories from that day resurface. The day that changed her life forever. *Guilt* along with grief. Gracie was supposed to be on that plane with her parents, but a cold had kept her home.

A female flight attendant close to Gracie's age smiled and greeted them, and if she noticed Gracie's look of fear, she said nothing. As the woman cast warm glances at the twins, she questioned. "Have they flown before?" She assumed Max and Trixie were Gracie's children. *Oh, how she wished.*

"Yes. They flew with their father about a year ago." She'd somehow remembered what Brianna had told her over the phone, which in itself was a wonder.

The flight attendant beamed as she gently patted Trixie's head. "Ah, seasoned travelers. Very good. I hope you all will have a wonderful flight. It won't be a long one."

Nodding her thanks, Gracie led the children halfway down the aisle to their seats. She hoped there wouldn't be an argument over who sat next to the window. To her great relief, Max was agreeable to let his sister have the window seat and he sat in the aisle seat. Gracie sat in the middle, in hopes she could offer attention equally to both children. As she clicked their seatbelts and was about to take out a book she'd brought along for them, she heard sniffles. Trixie's tears cascaded down her cheeks.

"What's the matter, sweetheart?"

"I forgot Roscoe. R-Roscoe's at home." More tears accompanied by her small shoulders shaking.

Gracie's heart melted. Trixie had left her favorite stuffed animal at home, and Gracie hadn't thought to mention the toy as she'd grabbed up a few items the children would need, in addition to locating their birth certificates in a file cabinet. She knew how special that toy rabbit was to the child, because she remembered Trixie taking Roscoe with them to get a Christmas tree.

With her thoughts diverted from her own fear to Trixie's problem, Gracie patted her arm and leaned closer. "I'm so sorry we didn't bring Roscoe, but you know what? I'm sure that Roscoe wanted to stay home and keep an eye on your Christmas tree." Gracie spoke in a serious tone, and Trixie's crying ceased and she gazed up in wonder.

"He did? Roscoe wanted to stay with our Christmas tree?"

Gracie nodded with enthusiasm. "Oh yes, I know he did. Even though Pedro is staying in your kitchen with food and water and not in the living room near the tree, Roscoe was still concerned that the tree might somehow fall over. So he wanted to make sure it is still beautiful when you get home." She nodded with certainty, more than a little relieved that her hastily thought-up story had actually comforted the child. Not to mention calming Gracie's own fears.

Just when she had convinced herself she could get through this flight, the plane began moving. Faster and faster, it taxied down the runway, preparing to lift up into the sky. Terror threatened to consume her and she bit her bottom lip to keep from crying out. Would her heart burst? Images of her parents' faces flashed through her mind as tears welled in her eyes. She squeezed the armrests, digging her fingernails into them. *I can do all things through Christ which strengtheneth me.* She recited the comforting Bible verse over and over in her head as she felt the jet lifting upward.

"Miss Gracie, that was fun!" Max looked up at her, his brown eyes wide with excitement.

Releasing a deep breath that she'd not realized she was holding, Gracie gazed down at the precious, dark-haired little boy seated to her left. His happy, trusting face did something to her racing heart, and Gracie knew then that they would all be okay. Despite her extreme fear, panic, and anxiety. *Thank you, Lord.* She never would've imagined that God would use small children to help her overcome the gripping fear that had consumed her the past few years. She released another long, slow breath.

Now if only Blake would get well so he could return home to Florida. That would be the focus of her prayers for the remainder of the flight. But first she leaned toward Max and tweaked his nose. "I'm glad you're enjoying this, sweetie." Gracie turned to

Trixie, who'd been unusually quiet. She obviously didn't enjoy the plane's takeoff as her brother had, because she was pale.

"Are you feeling okay, sweetheart?"

Tilting her head toward Gracie, Trixie nodded. "But I don't like the plane to go so fast."

Gracie patted her arm gently as she agreed with her. "But you know what? We'll be having a snack soon, and then before we know it, we'll be landing and you and Max can see your dad." Although she intended the comment to reassure the child, Trixie's face scrunched in worry.

"Is Daddy gonna be okay, Miss Gracie? When you were on the phone with Aunt Brianna, you said he's sick. I don't want him to die." Her dark eyes brimmed with tears as her bottom lip trembled.

Max looked over at his sister, then up at Gracie. "Why is Trixie cryin'?"

Drawing in a deep breath as she again prayed—this time for wisdom in caring for these children—Gracie pasted on a bright smile. "Trixie is worried about your dad since he's sick, but I have an idea. Why don't we pray to Jesus? We can pray that your dad will get well soon."

"Sometimes we say prayers at preschool." Trixie's comment made Gracie wonder if the children ever had prayer times with their father at home.

"That's special, Trixie. Praying is just talking to Jesus, because He always hears us."

Trixie nodded and the tears stopped.

"Okay, let's bow our heads for a minute and whisper up a prayer for Jesus to help your dad get well soon." Gracie's heart melted as she looked at each twin and saw their little heads bowed and lips moving. She quickly offered up her own prayer.

Dear Lord, please let Blake recover from whatever is going on with his health. These precious children have lost one parent, and I don't know if they could handle losing another one.

~ ~ ~

Who had placed sandbags on his eyes? That had to be why he couldn't open his eyelids all the way. Why was he so groggy? Blake struggled yet again to open his eyes and see where he was. Searching his fuzzy brain, he attempted to remember what had happened to him. The last thing he recalled was stepping onto the hotel elevator to head back up to his room. And now—he had no idea where he was or what had happened. As if a heavy fog covered him, he gave in and let his eyes close again.

A gentle female voice spoke to him sometime later. "Mr. Donovan? Can you open your eyes for me? I need to check your vital signs."

Vital signs? Was he in a doctor's office? He managed to open his eyes and squinted into the kind face of a middle-aged nurse. She gave him a motherly smile and briefly explained he'd had a ruptured appendix.

"Apparently your pain was so severe you

blacked out, so paramedics were called and you were rushed here to the hospital."

"My kids." Blake weakly murmured the words.

"Your relatives were notified. Another nurse told me it was your sister."

Oh no. Poor Brianna must be frantic if they phoned her. But the nurse's next words sent sheer panic coursing through him and caused him to wonder what he'd done.

"You were calling out about your children— insistent that they be brought to you. That information was relayed to the relative. Again, I'm assuming it was your sister." The nurse patted his arm and offered another comforting smile. "Now don't worry about anything. I'm sure this is frightening for you, but your surgery went well, and you'll be back to normal in no time. Let me take your vital signs and see if the doctor has ordered more medicine for you." She fastened the blood pressure cuff to his arm and proceeded to check his signs.

Blake tried to nod, but his mind was still absorbing what she'd said. He had called out about Max and Trixie and insisted they be brought to him? They were in Florida, and he was in South Carolina. At least he assumed he still was—after this ordeal he wasn't certain about anything. Trying his best to replay what had happened after he blacked out on the elevator was futile. The only thing he remembered was stepping onto the elevator and hearing someone calling his name.

The nurse informed him that his vital signs were good. "Now you just rest while I check your chart and see if you need any meds. You're going to be fine, Mr. Donovan. And by the way, my name is Nancy Strain, but everyone calls me Nurse Nancy. I'll be back shortly, so just relax."

Blake gave in to his drowsy state and let his eyes close. He wasn't sure how long he dozed but later was awakened by the same nurse, telling him that he'd be due some medicine within the hour. Then she leaned a bit closer and whispered, "And I have a message to give you from your sister. She said your twins are on their way, so please don't worry." She patted his arm and before Blake could ask a coherent question, she exited the room.

Had he heard correctly? Did the nurse say his children were heading to see him? Since they couldn't travel alone, maybe Bri was coming with them. Oh, what a lot of trouble he was causing for his family.

He closed his eyes again but couldn't sleep. His children were probably terrified, knowing he was sick. Not to mention the fact that Christmas was fast approaching. He still needed to buy toys for the twins and help them decorate the tree. He'd promised them their first Christmas in their beach home would be special. *Yeah, right.*

Opening his eyes, he gazed around the sterile-looking room. How had he gotten to this point? Stuck in a job he didn't like, stuck on a business trip he didn't want to take, and now stuck in a hospital instead of at home with his kids. Despair washed over him and he sighed, only to be reminded by a jolting pain that he'd recently had surgery. If he and God were on better terms, this is definitely a time he'd pray. But there was no way the Almighty would listen to him now, was there?

The nurse whisked into his room, as perky as she'd been earlier. "Here you go, Mr. Donovan. Meds to help you feel better. From the expression on your face, I'm assuming you've had some pain, am I correct?"

Blake nodded.

After assessing the level of his pain, the nurse handed him a small cup of water as he swallowed the tablets.

"I'll bet you're eager to see your children. How old are they?"

"Five-year-old twins. A boy and a girl."

"Oh, how sweet. What a fun Christmas this will be." She beamed at him.

Blake attempted to muster a smile. "Yeah. This surgery is lousy timing."

"You know, the Lord has a reason for everything, and His timing is always perfect. So you keep the faith and just see how well things work out." Her eyes seemed to twinkle, causing Blake to wonder if he was dreaming this entire conversation.

After getting a feeble nod from her patient, Nurse Nancy exited the room.

Alone with his thoughts, he pondered her words. *Keep the faith.* Maybe that was his problem. He had no faith—not any more. Could that be at least part of his problem these past three years since Lorie's passing? He'd been bitter because of his situation, even though he dearly loved his precious children. He'd blamed his discontent on his job, but maybe it was more than his work.

The pain medicine was kicking in, because once again his eyelids felt weighted down and he gave in to sleep. *Gracie and his children were walking on the beach. They were laughing and having fun as he tried to catch up to them. But they were enjoying themselves so much they didn't appear to notice him. He ran and ran...and finally caught up to them. Gracie looked at him and smiled. He wanted to tell her he loved her, but he couldn't seem to speak.*

"Mr. Donovan! Are you ready to wake up now?" Nurse Nancy stood beside his bed, smiling curiously down at him.

His mind was still muddled from his dream, yet it was so real. He tried to open his eyes wider and manage a coherent look for his nurse. "Yes." He uttered the word weakly, wondering why he'd been awakened from that dream. Although it was just as well, because what if he told Gracie he loved her and she laughed at him? *It was a dream. A silly dream, that's all.*

Nurse Nancy laughed. "Are you sure you're awake? You must've been in a pretty deep sleep from that medicine."

Yes, that's why he'd had such a crazy dream— the pain medicine caused it. He nodded at his nurse so she'd know he was awake.

"I'm glad, because you have visitors. Very special visitors." There was that sparkle in her eyes again. What was going on? Had Bri and his children arrived?

Just as the nurse headed toward the door, it opened slowly and his twins stepped hesitantly into the room. Gracie was between his children and they each clasped a hand tightly.

Gracie. Looking even more beautiful than he'd remembered, although he'd seen her a few days ago.

He couldn't help noticing his children remained close to her, rather than running to his bedside. Most likely due to his appearance—after all, he must look vastly different from the dad they were accustomed to seeing. "Hey there—I'm glad to see you." Although directing the comment to his children, he was glad to see Gracie too, but wished he didn't look quite so rough. "Is Brianna with you?" Now he was confused as to why his neighbor had accompanied his children on a flight. Was Brianna okay?

Gracie stepped a little closer and smiled at him. "Brianna will explain everything when you get home, but she had car trouble and is stranded at the hospital with your cousin. They're waiting on the baby to arrive."

"Daddy, are you still sick?" Trixie's worried tone made him long to take her into his arms and give her a comforting hug. Since that was impossible, he'd have to do his best to assure his children he would be okay.

"I was very sick, Trixie, but didn't know what was wrong. I had an operation, so I'll be all better and we can have a nice Christmas." He reached out his hand toward Max, wanting to make certain his son wasn't distraught. As he ruffled Max's hair, the child grinned in his usual way, giving him a huge sense of relief.

"Miss Gracie flied on the plane with us, daddy." Max spoke softly.

Blake met Gracie's gaze. He was about to thank her, but Trixie spoke up with words that jolted him to his core.

"We prayed for you, daddy. On the plane ride me and Max and Miss Gracie all prayed for you to feel gooder." She beamed proudly.

Tears trickled down Blake's cheeks. His precious children and his kind, beautiful neighbor had prayed for him as they flew to be with him. Was God using messengers to reach Blake and draw him close? Earlier the nurse had mentioned God, and now he learned his children and Gracie had prayed for him.

As he softly thanked Trixie, Max, and Gracie for the prayers, his heart was softening. It was time—no, it was *past* time—to get on good terms with God again. He'd heard about miracles happening at Christmas time, and now he couldn't help but wonder if he was experiencing a Christmas miracle of his own.

~ ~ ~

Gracie's pulse raced as she watched Blake in his hospital bed. The poor guy must be miserable—not to mention embarrassed at his unkempt appearance. But he'd been through surgery, and no one looked good after that. But what caused her pulse to race was that even lying in a hospital bed, with an unshaven face and mussed hair, Blake Donovan was still incredibly handsome.

An awkward feeling swept over Gracie as she stood eight feet away from him, seeing the love in his eyes for his precious twins. Should she leave the room?

"Have a seat, Gracie. That chair might not be the best, but you can sit." His attempt at a grin did something to her insides.

She nodded and sat, still observing him with the twins. At that moment Trixie turned and looked at her, then came over and squeezed into the chair with Gracie. "Max, would you like to join us?" He shyly approached, perching on the other side of the chair.

Blake gazed over at them. "You all look cozy in that chair together. Too bad I don't have my camera." He began chuckling but quickly grimaced. "Ouch, it hurts to laugh." His face scrunched in pain.

"I'm sorry. Try not to laugh." Yet Gracie was glad they'd given him something to laugh about, because he must be uncomfortable. Her cell phone buzzed, so she grabbed it from her handbag and answered. Brianna's voice came through, wanting an update on her brother.

The two women talked a few minutes, and Blake motioned for the children to step to his bedside again. Gracie could overhear him asking about their flight.

When her call ended, Gracie informed Blake of the details Brianna had worked out. "Your sister will fly up and take the twins back to Florida. She said I can either fly back with them or remain here with you for the drive home. Your boss has contacted Brianna to tell her that he's arranged for a rental car so you won't have to fly so soon after surgery." She paused to take a breath. "But she's unsure if you'll be able to drive, so she asked if I'd be willing to drive the rental car for you." Gracie's head swam as she absorbed Brianna's plans. On a positive note, if she drove Blake home in a rental car, she wouldn't need to fly. *And I'd be spending lots of time with Blake.* She hoped he and the twins didn't hear her thumping heart. The thought of a long car ride with him would at least be an opportunity to learn more about him.

She mustered a smile as she awaited his decision. When he answered seconds later, her face heated in a crimson blush.

"Are you kidding? Try to drive myself after surgery or have a beautiful auburn-haired chauffeur?" His eyes held a teasing glint, which didn't help her blushing one bit.

She cleared her throat, wondering if his pain medication was causing his complimentary speech. "Okay, I'm fine with driving you, as long as your doctor gives you the okay to travel. And I'll stop the car as often as needed." Mentally calculating details, she was thankful it was the weekend, which meant she wasn't missing work. Plus she'd left plenty of food and water for her cats, so they should be fine until she returned home.

Max peered up at Gracie with questioning eyes. "You're not flying with us, Miss Gracie?"

She reached out and gently squeezed his little hand. "No, sweetie, but your Aunt Brianna will be flying with you and Trixie. I'll need to drive your dad home. But I'll see you again very soon. We still have lots of Christmas cookies to bake." She winked at him, pleased with his satisfied smile.

A few minutes later Gracie took the twins to the hospital cafeteria for a snack to give Blake time to rest. Hopefully, Brianna's suggested plans would work out—for all of them. Poor Brianna would be exhausted, flying up to South Carolina, seeing her brother and getting the twins, then flying back to Florida. But she was young and energetic.

About six o'clock that evening, Trixie squealed. "There's Aunt Bri!" She pointed toward a hallway off the small lobby where they were sitting while Blake napped. As his sister rushed toward them, the twins engulfed her in a hug, and then—to Gracie's surprise—Brianna stepped over and gave her a hug.

"You are a lifesaver, Gracie. I don't know what we would've done without you." She plopped onto a padded chair in the lobby as the twins hovered beside her. Gracie took the chair next to Brianna and they talked non-stop for the next fifteen minutes, discussing Blake's surgery, their flights, and the plan for Gracie to drive

Blake home to Florida. "That's going to be a long drive. Are you sure you don't mind?" Brianna's face held concern.

"No, it'll be fine. I've already told Blake that we'll stop as often as he needs to, if riding becomes too uncomfortable for him. I can pull off the road and he can stand for a little bit if needed."

"You're the best, Gracie. You really are." She squeezed Gracie's hand.

With a tired giggle, Gracie shrugged. "I guess I needed a little excitement in my normally-calm life, so this adventure provided it. I just hate that your brother had to have surgery."

"Yeah, when he gets well, I'm sure my mom will lecture him about taking better care of his health and not ignoring warning signs. He's admitted he'd been having pains in his side but thought they were caused by digestive issues." Brianna shook her head.

After Max commented he was hungry again, Gracie gasped. "I've lost track of time. I'm sure you children are hungry." She and Brianna accompanied the twins to the hospital cafeteria, where Brianna insisted on paying for the four meals. Eating restored some energy to Gracie, and she felt a bit perkier as they returned to the waiting area on Blake's floor.

A few minutes later, Nurse Nancy stepped into the small lobby area and beckoned them. "Mr. Donovan is asking for you all." She smiled at the group, but her eyes lingered on Gracie. As they headed to Blake's room, the nurse gently tugged Gracie's arm and whispered. "I'm not prying, but are you and Mr. Donovan…um, dating? You'd sure make a cute couple."

Gracie's hand flew to her mouth as an embarrassed grin formed. "We're neighbors and have become friends." What else could she say?

Nancy arched her eyebrows and placed a hand on her hip. "Well, it's the Christmas season, and special things happen during this time of year. So don't be surprised." She clamped her lips together, winked, and headed into a patient's room.

Exhausted, Gracie was eager to get a hotel room and sleep. Preferably for at least twelve hours—which would be totally unheard of for her. After visiting with Blake for a few minutes, she, Brianna, and the twins headed to a nearby hotel within walking distance of the hospital.

"That hospital receptionist highly recommended this hotel, and said they offer good rates for people staying there to be close to family in the hospital. We definitely qualify." Brianna shot her a playful gaze.

Since Gracie wasn't part of Blake's family, she figured Brianna was including her to be kind. To her relief everything at the hotel went smoothly, and the night manager even helped with their bags. Quickly hugging the twins and telling Brianna good-night, Gracie entered her simple but clean room, prepared for bed, and collapsed.

But before giving in to sleep, she wondered what the next day would hold as she drove Blake back to Coastal Breeze. Would the drive be awkward, or would he sleep most of the time? Surely this would be an opportunity to learn more about her handsome neighbor and get to know him better. But what if she discovered her first impressions of him had been accurate—that he didn't care about her at all?

~ ~ ~

The next day seemed to pass in a whirlwind as Gracie, Brianna, and the twins checked out of the hotel. Shortly afterward, Blake was discharged from the hospital, and they began their trips home to Florida. A shuttle van carried Brianna and the children to the airport, and Blake's boss had a rental car ready at the hospital. Gracie uttered a silent prayer of thanks, knowing there could've been glitches in their plans with the rental car or Blake's hospital discharge. Yet everything went smoothly.

Once the drive to Florida began, Gracie lifted one more prayer for safe travels, adding a quick request for her time with Blake to go well without awkward moments.

"Are you sure you're okay with this? It's a long drive from here to Coastal Breeze." Blake peered over at her from the passenger seat of the rental car. He'd been able to shave and comb his hair, so now he appeared back to his normal self, except for a slower gait.

"I'm fine with driving. As long as you trust me behind the wheel." She grinned, hoping to keep things light for the trip ahead.

"Uh-oh, I should've checked your driving record, I guess. Remember, I've just had surgery and am still recuperating." His teasing tone was a good sign.

Their playful banter continued. "I'll have you know my driving record is excellent. So you just sit back and relax. But please do let me know whenever you need to stop." Gracie kept her focus on the road ahead.

Surprisingly, the miles sped by and the time passed quicker than she'd expected. Blake dozed off and on, only asking to stop a few times during the entire drive. When he was awake, their conversation flowed easily, and he opened up to Gracie about changing careers.

"My Aunt Bonnie has reminded me that life is short and it's important to be happy in what we're doing. Which is why I left my home in Georgia to relocate to the Florida panhandle for my job. Now I have no regrets at all." Gracie could feel Blake's eyes on her as she drove.

"That's good to hear. I'd be worried if you regretted your move due to lousy neighbors." He released a wry chuckle.

"Are you kidding? My neighbors are the best." *Okay, don't overdo it. Maybe I'd better let him do the talking.* She could tell he was still staring at her.

"It just so happens that your neighbors are pretty crazy about you, too. And not just the young neighbors."

Gracie wondered if she needed to pull off the road, because his comment and frequent stares caused her heart to pound. She gripped the steering wheel so tightly her knuckles were hurting. What was wrong with her? *Calm down, Gracie. It's probably his pain meds making him say those things.* Yet she couldn't help wondering if maybe he *was* trying to let her know he was as attracted to her as she was to him.

"Okay, according to that sign, we don't even have fifty miles left. I think we've made good time on our drive." As she switched their conversation topic, Gracie could feel fatigue catching up with her.

"Yeah, we have made good time today. And considering I've had surgery recently, I've actually had a good time." Blake's tone was sincere.

All she could do was offer a weak smile and nod, keeping her eyes straight ahead. Did this man realize how he affected her? Not only his presence in the car, but now his words. Could it be that Blake Donovan really cared for her? She didn't have to wait long to learn the answer.

~ ~ ~

Blake knew it wasn't his medication causing him to open up to her. No, he needed to finally admit his true feelings for Gracie Norton, because he'd been suppressing them for weeks. She was caring, beautiful, and his kids adored her. *He* adored her too, and it was time to do something about his feelings.

"Um…the twins have been asking if you could

do more activities with us. What do you think?" *That was really romantic, Donovan. What woman could resist that?* His silent chiding made him want to slide down in his seat, which was impossible. His pain was beginning to bother him again, so he'd better sit still.

When they stopped at a traffic light in Destin, Gracie shifted to look at him. "So the twins want to spend more time with me. That's very nice." She turned back to focus on the road.

Her tone held a slight edge. Blake hoped she was just being playful with him and that he hadn't blown it. "Well, the twins aren't the only ones. Their dad wants to spend more time with you. A lot more time." There. He'd said it. The proverbial ball was in her court, so he'd see how she felt. As his mother had reminded him years ago, nothing ventured, nothing gained.

Soon they were at another traffic light stop. She turned to him again, this time smiling. In fact, she appeared to be glowing as she spoke. "I'd really like that." The light turned green so she continued driving. For the remainder of their ride, they sat in silence, and Blake was okay with that.

Darkness descended and as they drew closer to Coastal Breeze, colorful Christmas lights seemed to welcome them back home. They passed a Christmas tree lot and Blake was relieved he'd already bought their tree.

Minutes later Gracie pulled the rental car into Blake's driveway. "Home sweet home."

She proclaimed and turned off the engine.

Blake unfastened his seatbelt, reached toward her and squeezed her hand. "Thank you for everything. For flying to South Carolina with the twins and being so wonderful. And for driving me home today." He hesitated. "And remember I'm going to reimburse you for everything, just as Brianna told you. The flight, the hotel, your food, everything."

Gracie lowered her head before looking directly into his eyes. "That's not necessary, Blake. I won't go into my past now...but having no choice but to step onto that plane yesterday helped me overcome something major in my life. But more importantly, spending time with Max and Trixie was..." Her words trailed off as moisture pooled in her green eyes. Even in the darkness, Blake could see the tears. He gently reached up to her face to brush away a drop that slid down her cheek.

"Gracie? Are you okay?" Why was she crying? Had he upset her somehow?

She nodded and an embarrassed-sounding giggle escaped. "I'm s-sorry. I didn't mean to get so emotional, but I was trying to say that being with your twins was priceless. Those children are treasures, Blake. I'm sure you realize that. But I've grown to love them, which sounds silly since we're not even related."

Blake leaned closer, ignoring the pain. "No, it doesn't sound silly. That's just another reason I have feelings for you, Gracie. I haven't known you very long, but you've always been so caring and attentive to my children and they adore you. I think they were drawn to you the first time they met you." He paused and cleared his throat. "The truth is, I was too, but didn't want to admit it." He hesitated only a few seconds and plunged ahead. "You see, even before my late wife became sick, our marriage wasn't good. But the twins were so young and we thought we needed to stay together. Then Lorie's cancer diagnosis came, which was terrible. I remained with her, of course, doing all I could." He took a deep breath, thankful that he hadn't shocked Gracie with his revelation. "Since I've been widowed, a couple of well-meaning friends have arranged dates for me, but those bombed." He laughed and shrugged.

"I'm so sorry about your late wife—I can't imagine what you've been through. But you're doing a great job with your children." She offered a sweet smile before opening her door.

Blake opened his door and moved as quickly as possible to come around to her side, hating the pain that was flaring up. He'd take more medicine when he was in his house, but now he had something more important to do.

As the couple stood beside the car, Blake thanked her again for all her help. Then he leaned in and placed a sweet, lingering kiss on her lips. Not too long, but more than a hasty peck. Thankfully, she didn't resist.

When the kiss ended, they remained silent for a few seconds, staring at each other. Then Blake caught movement from the corner of his eye and realized his sister was standing on his front porch, waving at them. "Guess we'd better get inside. Do you want me to walk you to your door since it's dark? I'll be glad to do that."

Gracie thanked him but declined his offer. "I'll be fine. I'll get my luggage and head home."

Brianna stepped out to the car to greet them and told Blake to be quiet inside the house. "I finally got the twins to sleep, even though they wanted to wait up for you both." After helping Gracie lift the luggage from the rental car's trunk, she looked at her with a wide smile. Then Brianna threw her arms around Gracie in a warm hug. "You are amazing. Helping us out on a moment's notice." She turned and peered at Blake. "This lady is a jewel, big brother."

Blake couldn't agree more. And he would do everything he could to make her part of their lives. Forever.

~ ~ ~

Chapter 8

Gracie's mind whirled like the pinwheels she'd bought the twins at the fall festival only weeks earlier. How had so much happened since then?

"Miss Gracie! Look at Cheddar and Tubby under the Christmas tree." Trixie's giggles cut into her musings.

Brushing the flour from her hands, Gracie hurried into her living room. She couldn't suppress a chuckle because her two felines appeared to think they belonged underneath her tree. To her relief the cats hadn't bothered any gifts or ornaments—so far.

"They look like furry presents. Would you like to help me with the cookies now?" Gracie felt that maternal tug she often had with the twins.

Minutes later, she and Trixie talked and laughed as they cut festive shapes in the sugar cookie dough. Her heart warmed as the child chatted about her brother.

"I'm making a reindeer cookie for Max. He likes animals a lot." Before Gracie could comment, Trixie gazed thoughtfully up at her. "You like animals a lot too, right?"

"I sure do. In fact, one day I'd like to have some land where I could keep some animals that need a home. I'd still have Tubby and Cheddar in my house, but it would be nice to have room for extra animals."

Trixie appeared to be absorbing this information.

"That's nice that Max and your dad are running errands together. But I'm happy you stayed here to help me bake." Gracie didn't miss the pleased glow on her face.

After taking the last batch of cookies from the oven, Gracie grabbed her ringing cell phone. Blake's voice sent her heart into a flutter as it often did.

"Hi. Max and I picked up a barbecue meal for all of us, if you girls want to join us over here." His voice sounded upbeat.

"Would it work for you and Max to bring the food here? Trixie has been an angel helping me bake lots of cookies, so that can be our dessert."

Ten minutes later the foursome sat at Gracie's table. Max grinned sheepishly, with barbecue sauce around his mouth, as he told about visiting the gift shop. "We got Christmas presents, but Dad says I can't tell what they are." His eyes darted to Gracie and Trixie before he focused on his sandwich again.

Blake laughed. "Good boy. We want the presents to be surprises for your sister and Miss Gracie." His playful smile made Gracie's heart do a little tap dance.

"Something else happened while we were in the gift shop." His eyes glowed. "The owner, Ginny Grover, asked if I knew anyone looking for a job. I figured she was joking since it's close to Christmas, but we got to talking and it turns out her niece's husband, Thomas, is looking for someone to share his workload. He works for a successful company called Coastal Industries, and apparently their business has skyrocketed." He paused and shook his head as if in disbelief. "That entire conversation with Ginny was amazing since I've been wanting to change careers. I know this might not work out, but she gave me Thomas's contact information and will mention my name to him. It's a long shot, but I figure it's worth talking to him to see what the job entails." Blake took a swig of tea.

"That's wonderful. I'll pray the Lord will show you what to do about your job. You never know—this might work out. I don't know Thomas well, but I've seen him at church, and he seems very nice. And I know he and his wife, Emma, are expecting a baby anytime now, so I'm sure he needs help with his work."

Blake thanked her for the prayers. Seconds later Trixie spoke, and Gracie almost dropped her bite of barbecue.

"We're like a family, daddy. You, Max, me, and Miss Gracie all together." She stated her observation matter-of-factly before popping a French fry into her mouth.

Gracie held her breath, unsure of Blake's response. To her surprise he nodded. "Yes, Trixie. We are like a family." He sent a secretive glance across the table to Gracie, causing her to choke on her tea. Quickly dabbing her mouth, she mumbled a comment about eating too fast.

After supper the twins played with the cats in the living room, laughing while Tubby and Cheddar pounced on toy mice. Blake assisted Gracie in the kitchen with the clean-up.

"Thank you for the meal—it was delicious. I've already packaged some Christmas cookies for you to take home. There's plenty if you need to take some when you visit your family on Christmas." A melancholy cloud descended over her as she was reminded she would be alone that day. She ignored it and busily wiped the counter, but realized Blake was smiling at her.

"Um…Gracie, you haven't mentioned having special plans for Christmas, but the kids and I would love for you to join us if you'd like. I realize you haven't met any of my family except Brianna, but I promise everyone is nice and would welcome you. And I may as well admit that Bri thinks you're wonderful." He gazed at her, a look of expectancy in his dark eyes.

Gracie paused with the dishcloth in her hand. "What?"

He laughed. "I'm inviting you to join us for Christmas at Brianna's. If you'd rather not, it's okay." His downcast expression said otherwise.

"Anyway, I don't want to put you on the spot, so you can let me know later, if you'd like. But..." His voice trailed off for a moment before he drew in a deep breath and continued. "We would really like for you to join us. In fact, Trixie and Max both have been asking if you could be with us on Christmas."

"Are they the only ones who want me to join you all?" She couldn't resist a teasing comment.

He stepped closer, took the dishcloth from her hands and placed it on the counter. Before Gracie had time to analyze what was happening, Blake placed a brief but sweet kiss on her lips. Giggles erupted from the doorway leading to the living room. The twins stood there with hands over their mouths as if they'd just witnessed something funny. Yet they appeared pleased with what they'd seen.

Gracie knew her face was crimson and she couldn't hide, so she laughed and made the only comment she could muster. "I knew I forgot to get some mistletoe. Thank you for reminding me."

Blake wore a mischievous grin and nodded. "Happy to help."

Trixie had contained her giggles and stepped closer to Blake. "Daddy, are you going to marry Miss Gracie? Max and me likes her."

Gracie froze. How would Blake respond?

Although he appeared as startled by the comment as Gracie was, he casually replied. "We will see, Trixie. Now, you and Max play for a few more minutes with Tubby and

Cheddar, while I make sure Miss Gracie has some cookies ready for us to carry home." He winked at both twins, who happily returned to playing with the cats.

Not wanting things to become more awkward, Gracie changed the topic completely. "Did I tell you I'm the maid of honor in my best friend's wedding? It's this next weekend in Panama City, where her parents live. She wants me to stay at their home the entire weekend, so I'll leave plenty of food and water for my kitties while I'm gone." Was she rambling from nervousness? She glanced up at Blake, who gave a smiling nod.

"Wow, you've got a full weekend planned, and it sounds special. I hope everything goes well for your friend."

"Yes, it should. Kira and her family are very excited, and they've been working on the plans for a while. I'm really close to them, and they've always welcomed me as though I was part of their family." She paused and shook her head. "Even Kira's younger brother has always joked with me a lot, and it's been fun since I didn't have siblings." She smiled as images of Kira's brother and his pranks flitted through her mind. "Anyway, it should be a fun weekend, and after that I'll finish getting ready for Christmas."

Blake eased closer and now he leaned in, whispering. "When I purchase some toys for the twins, would you mind keeping them hidden here until Christmas? I don't want to take any chances on presents being discovered before Christmas day."

"I'd be honored. Just let me know when you have the toys. I have an extra closet where the presents will be safely hidden." She offered a conspiratorial grin, tickled that he wanted to include her in helping.

After Blake and the twins returned home, Gracie sat at her kitchen table to address a few Christmas cards. With the wedding the following weekend and then Christmas, she needed to make the most of her free time this weekend. Yet now her house seemed quiet—too quiet. She missed the laughter and voices of the twins. *You miss their father being here too.* Yes, she had to admit that being with Blake's family gave her a special feeling—a feeling she could easily get accustomed to—every day.

~ ~ ~

"How many days till Christmas, daddy?" Trixie asked Blake yet again the following Saturday.

He grinned as he told her. "And no peeking at presents under our Christmas tree. We'll open everything on Christmas morning." He attempted a stern tone and look, but with his sweet twins it was difficult. Their innocent excitement was contagious.

As he wiped oatmeal off Max's face, the child looked up with a puzzled expression in his dark eyes. "Miss Gracie said she's a maid in a wedding. Will she hafta mop?"

Suppressing a hearty laugh so as not to hurt his son's feelings, Blake explained Gracie's role as the maid of honor in her friend's wedding. Max nodded and seemed to understand.

Throughout the weekend, Blake couldn't stop thinking about Gracie and visualized how she would look as a bridesmaid. *Or a bride.* He needed to rein in those thoughts because he should be focusing on his upcoming career change. But he was eager to update Gracie on his interview with Thomas Wilton. It boggled his mind that a chance conversation with Ginny Grover in the gift shop could lead to a job.

On Sunday afternoon, Blake was looking over the Coastal Industries information Thomas had emailed when he heard the slam of a car door. The twins were playing in their rooms, so he stepped to the living room window to glance out—but then wished he hadn't.

A black sports car had pulled into Gracie's driveway and a young man with broad shoulders was hoisting Gracie's luggage from the trunk. She stood near him, laughing and clutching a bouquet of red flowers that appeared to be roses. She looked radiant, and it was obvious she was enjoying the man's company. He leaned over to peck her on the cheek, and she giggled.

Blake's chest tightened. Yet he knew his eyes weren't playing tricks on him. Did Gracie have a date for her friend's wedding? It certainly appeared to be the case, and Blake didn't like it. *But you have no claims on her. You haven't even been on a real date with her.* So why did he feel he'd been deceived?

He checked on the twins and then prepared

clothes and snacks for the upcoming week. Clarity returned and he knew what he had to do. The next time he and Gracie spoke, he'd tell her there was no need to join them for Christmas. *Especially since she obviously has a beau in her life.* Blowing out a frustrated sigh, Blake returned to his computer to read the notes from Thomas regarding his new job. But it was no use. The screen was a blur as he tried to concentrate. The image of Gracie and the man in her driveway replayed in his head. He'd been a fool to think she had real feelings for him. She adored his children, but her feelings didn't include him.

~ ~ ~

On Monday at the animal clinic, Gracie stayed busy getting vital signs on pets, doing bloodwork, and assuring a couple of clients that their fur babies would be fine. She appreciated Dr. Tatum's compassion and the fact he referred to the pet owners as moms and dads. It was obvious the clients appreciated it too.

Dora was eager to hear about the wedding, so on their lunch break, Gracie shared details of Kira's ceremony and reception. "Her younger brother, Kevin, hasn't changed a bit, and he's still like the little brother I never had." She laughed while sharing a few funny moments from the previous weekend. "On the trip home on Sunday afternoon, he had me laughing so hard at his silly jokes." She shook her head playfully.

The remainder of the day Gracie's thoughts kept returning to the wedding weekend. Everything had been picture-perfect, and Kira's family made her feel special, like she was part of the family. Kira's dad even insisted on picking up Gracie Saturday morning, so she could leave her car at home. He'd jokingly told her their house would resemble a used-car lot with relatives visiting, so one less vehicle would be helpful. Gracie was blessed to be included in all the wedding festivities.

On Wednesday Gracie wondered when Blake would let her know about hiding toys for the twins. She'd cleared a space in her extra closet and was waiting to hear from him, yet there had been no communication. Hopefully no one was sick, but if she didn't hear from him by Friday she'd contact him.

After work that afternoon Gracie stepped to the curb to tie a bright red bow on her mailbox. She enjoyed adding festive holiday touches wherever she could, and since this was her first Christmas in Coastal Breeze, she wanted to continue her usual decorating traditions as she'd done in Georgia.

"Hey Miss Gracie!" Trixie's voice called to her from Blake's front door.

Her heart lifted at seeing the child, and she waved and returned the greeting. Stepping back to see how the bow looked on her mailbox, Gracie realized Pedro had been in the house with Trixie and was slipping past her out the door. In a flash the large dog came bounding toward her.

Trixie was squealing and running after the dog, who by now had run past Gracie into the street. Before Gracie could tell Trixie to stay in the yard, the little girl ran after her dog and into the path of an approaching car.

Gracie's heart hammered. She *must* protect Trixie! Lunging into the street between the car and Trixie, Gracie yelled for the car to stop. Tires squealed. Brakes screeched. Gracie lost her footing and flailed her arms to break the fall. She fought off the spots that appeared before her eyes and forced herself to raise her head. She ignored the searing pain in her hands that had grasped the rough pavement.

Where was Trixie? What happened to Trixie? She peered under the car.

~ ~ ~

Blake froze. From his front door, he watched in slow motion as his daughter, his dog, and his love converged in front of a moving car. His heart plummeted. His voice bellowed, "No-o-o!" Pushing open the storm door, he bounded toward the street. Where was Trixie? How badly was Gracie hurt? How could this be happening?

Trixie's sobs reached his ears, and he saw her huddled on the opposite side of the street, clutching Pedro. "Stay there, Trixie. I'm coming!" It appeared she was okay, so he had to check on Gracie. *Oh Lord, please let her be okay. She tried to save my daughter. Don't let anything happen to her.*

"Gracie! Gracie!" He crouched beside her, almost afraid to look.

The car's driver, a middle-aged man, stood by the bumper, his hand covering his mouth, his eyes terrified. Blake hoped the man wasn't in shock. "Is she okay? I'm so sorry...I tried to stop." The man spoke the words over and over.

Gracie slowly raised her head, a dazed look on her face. Her voice came out in a raspy whisper. "Trixie. Where is Trixie?" Tears filled her eyes.

Blake reached out to gently help her stand, cringing at seeing the blood on her hands where the pavement had torn away the skin. He ushered her to the edge of her yard. "Trixie and Pedro are fine. They're on the other side of the street and I'm going to get them." After rushing back across the street to get his daughter and the dog, Blake rejoined Gracie. The car's driver had joined them, still visibly shaken by what had happened.

"I'm so terribly sorry, ma'am. Are you okay? Do you need my insurance information? I feel awful about this."

Blake couldn't help feeling sorry for the man, although his top priority was seeing to Gracie right now.

Gracie nodded and assured him she'd be okay. "I lost my balance and went down on the pavement. Your car didn't hit me. It's only my hands that are hurt, and they'll heal."

Blake could tell that even in her dazed state of mind, Gracie was doing her best to reassure the man. As the driver returned to his car to leave,

Blake hugged Trixie, then told her to keep a firm hold on Pedro's leash and take him inside the house. Blake took Gracie's arm and escorted her into his house.

A pale, scared Max stood inside the front door, so Blake took time to assure him that Trixie, Miss Gracie, and Pedro were all okay. "I need you to pick up your toys in the living room, and don't let Pedro out of your sight." He spoke firmly to his children and the dog, who had a guilty glint in his eyes.

As his children followed his instructions, Blake told Gracie to come with him to the kitchen. "We need to get your hands cleaned and bandaged. I'm afraid they'll be sore for a few days." He was relieved she didn't insist on returning to her house yet.

"Are you sure you don't need to go to the hospital and be checked?" He tenderly began cleaning her wounded hands, being as careful as he could and knowing it must be terribly painful for her. "Are you sure nothing else hurts?"

She gave him a sweet smile and weakly shook her head. "No, I don't need to go to the hospital. I'm a bit shaken, but I'll be all right."

The twins stood in the living room, peering into the kitchen to observe Blake and Gracie.

Blake knew they must still be worried about Gracie, so he turned to them as he gently dried Gracie's hands. "Miss Gracie will be okay. I'm going to put medicine on her hands to help them feel better. You can get some books from your rooms, but then sit in the living room." Both children nodded solemnly.

"I'm glad I bought a first-aid kit a while back. I know it has some gauze bandages and ointment, so you sit here and I'll be right back."

Minutes later, Blake had coated Gracie's hands with ointment and lovingly bandaged them, fighting the urge to kiss her as he did so. He only hoped the ointment would relieve some of the pain in her hands.

As he escorted her back to the living room, Blake thought about what had just happened. Witnessing not only his child and dog but the woman he cared deeply about in trouble shook him to his core. Suddenly the fact that she'd had a date with someone else didn't matter. Guilt for keeping his distance the past three days poked at him, but he couldn't dwell on that right now.

Trixie rushed up to Gracie and hugged her legs, tears streaming down her face. "I'm sorry, Miss Gracie." With trembling lips, the child repeated the words, remorse evident in her features.

Gracie sat on the sofa and gently pulled the child into her lap, being careful with her bandaged hands. "I know you were trying to catch Pedro, sweetie. But the street is a dangerous place, so you must never run into it." She smoothed Trixie's hair off her face and wiped the tears from her cheeks.

"Daddy, I'm hungry. Can Miss Gracie eat supper with us?" Max's comment reminded Blake it was time to eat and he'd prepared nothing. An idea quickly formed. "How about I order a pizza and Miss Gracie can eat with us?" He leaned toward Gracie. "If you like pizza." She responded with a smiling nod.

An hour later they were enjoying pizza and talking about Christmas. Pedro was back in the doghouse and given his supper, but no treats this time. He hung his head and avoided eye contact with his humans.

While the twins viewed a children's Christmas movie on television, Blake and Gracie remained at the table, sipping coffee Blake had brewed for them. In a lowered voice she questioned him about gifts for the twins.

Blake hung his head. "I owe you an apology for not contacting you this week. I've got their presents in my trunk but thought maybe you'd changed your mind about helping me."

A puzzled frown creased her brow. "Why would I change my mind? I love your twins."

Might as well open up. He drew in a deep breath. "I saw you arrive home from your friend's wedding on Sunday. With a date. So I figured you might not have much time for us." Why did he feel like a fool admitting this to her?

Gracie's face registered conflicting emotions. Confusion, hurt, and then a look of amazement. "My date? What date?" She began laughing and shaking her head. "You thought Kevin was my date? Now that's funny. He's Kira's little brother and has been like the brother I never had. Since Kira's dad had picked me up Saturday morning, her brother drove me home on Sunday afternoon. They're like family to me and insisted I spend the wedding weekend with them." She frowned, directing a stare at him with those spearmint green eyes. Eyes that could make him forget what was going on at the moment.

Now everything made sense. She hadn't been with a date, but Blake had been a fool and jumped to conclusions. Now he was the one shaking his head. "I'm sorry, Gracie. I shouldn't have assumed that guy was your date. But I'll admit it bothered me seeing you laughing with that guy. And then he kissed you on the cheek." *Just be quiet, Donovan. You're making this worse.*

Giggles sounded behind him, and Blake turned to see both children grinning. "What's going on?" He eyed Trixie, then Max.

"Me and Max want you to ask Miss Gracie." She covered her mouth and erupted in giggles, joined by Max.

"Ask Miss Gracie about what?" Blake's heart raced. Were his children referring to a proposal? He knew they adored Gracie and had even commented she'd be a good mommy, but Blake and his children had never discussed the possibility of his proposing to her.

Blake was stunned as Max was the one to answer his question. "To be our mommy." He clamped his little mouth shut as if that was all he could manage to say.

Gracie appeared as shocked as he was. Unsure what to say, Blake smiled at his children while his mind raced for a response. But before he could say anything, Trixie stepped closer and dug something from her pocket. "Here, daddy. This is the ring I got at the festival with Miss Gracie. She said she likes it, so that can be her wedding ring."

His mouth dropped open, but no words came out. He looked at Gracie, who had tears streaming down her face. Her eyes gazed at the children, then at him. The twins remained standing close by, and since Trixie had held the ring out, Blake carefully took it from her small hand. A golf ball-sized lump must be in his throat, because he could hardly swallow.

"Trixie, this is so sweet. Thank you."

She nodded before returning to the living room to continue watching the movie. Max trailed her.

Blake gazed across the table at Gracie, who was swiping tears away from her cheeks. "I'm not sure what just happened." He drew in a deep breath before forging ahead. "But I do know that the Lord uses my children to get through to me sometimes." He moved to the chair next to Gracie and gently took her bandaged hand in his. "We haven't known each other very long, but I do know that you're the kindest, most beautiful woman I've ever met. My children love you…and I do too. Will you marry me?"

Gracie gazed into his eyes, and her smile said it all. Then she nodded. "I love you too, Blake. And you might've noticed I love Max and Trixie too." She drew in a breath and answered him. "Yes, I'll marry you."

He took her left hand and slowly slid the toy ring onto her finger, being careful not to pull off the bandage on her palm. Amazingly, the sparkly ring fit. He whispered that he'd be purchasing a diamond for her, but he didn't want Trixie to be hurt if he didn't use her ring.

Gracie held her left hand close to her heart and shook her head. "I don't need a diamond. If I have you and the twins, that's enough."

Blake thought his heart might burst as he looked at the woman he loved. Why had he denied it? A thought struck him and he laughed. "You know, this is not how I expected to ever propose to anyone, but I've got to say it's original." He grinned as he patted her left hand and touched the toy ring.

"Sometimes the unexpected things in life are the best. I never expected to fall in love with my neighbor, but I have. And becoming a mother to the most precious twins in the world is something I didn't expect either. But the Lord knows what we need, and I couldn't be happier."

~ ~ ~

EPILOGUE

"Gracie, you're the most beautiful bride ever." Aunt Bonnie blinked away tears as she smoothed the cascading veil around Gracie's hair. "I know your parents are smiling down from Heaven." She gently hugged her niece as Uncle Fred beamed proudly. He was waiting to escort her down the aisle of the Coastal Breeze Church when the ceremony began.

"I'm so blessed to have you both in my life." Gracie smiled at her beloved aunt and uncle. Before she could say anything else, small hands tugged at her arm. There stood Max and Trixie, both adorable in their wedding attire. "Thank you for being in my wedding, and most of all, for letting me be your mommy now." She placed a kiss on each twin's head as they grinned shyly up at her.

Max wore a suit and tie and clutched a small satin pillow for the rings. Trixie wore a pink flower-girl dress and clutched a small basket of red rose petals she was eager to sprinkle in the aisle.

Brianna and Kira joined them, both looking lovely in their pink gowns. Each carried a nosegay of red roses. "A Valentine wedding is so romantic and sweet." Kira released a sigh. "You know I'm beyond thrilled for you."

As Gracie nodded and smiled at her best friend, Brianna squeezed her arm. "I'm so excited you'll be part of our family now!"

Before Gracie could respond, Aunt Bonnie signaled it was time to begin the ceremony, and Uncle Fred gently took Gracie's arm to escort her down the aisle. Slowly walking toward the altar, she sent a reassuring smile to the twins, then gazed lovingly at her groom. She still marveled that this was her wedding day.

The twins were perfect throughout the brief but sweet ceremony, and sniffles could be heard from many of the attendees as they observed the precious family, now made complete with Gracie as the wife and mother.

Afterwards, a reception was held in the large building where the fall festival had been. In October Gracie never would've imagined she would be a bride the following February. She appreciated so many members of the church attending—including Emma and Thomas Wilton, with their sweet baby girl, Holly, in tow. As Gracie admired the sleeping baby who'd been born just before Christmas, Emma leaned in closer. "You might have a baby to add to your precious family one day."

Dr. Tatum and the animal clinic employees were

in attendance, and they huddled around Gracie expressing their congratulations. Her boss commented about the couple's plans to live on land on the outskirts of Coastal Breeze. "Even though you'll be housing your own animals, I hope you'll continue working for me. I'd hate to lose such a valuable employee." He added a laugh as Dora nodded in agreement.

After Gracie assured Dr. Tatum she had no immediate plans to leave the animal clinic, Blake spoke up. "But later she may decide to be a full-time mom to both children and animals." He winked at his bride and they all laughed. Gracie was in awe that Blake had purchased a home on three acres, which would allow her room to house animals she planned to take in.

Midge Weatherbee rushed over to the couple, offering congratulations and eyeing them both with a twinkle in her eyes. "Gracie's aunt told me you're spending your honeymoon in her friend's mountain cabin. How romantic! She also said there's a stone fireplace—perfect for this time of year." She gave quick hugs to the bride and groom before scuttling away.

Minutes later, family gathered around the newlyweds. Bonnie made certain she'd given them the key to the cabin, as Fred teasingly admonished them to get on the road.

Blake leaned toward Gracie's ear. "I'm looking forward to enjoying that cabin with you, Mrs. Donovan." A tingle rushed through her at his words. *Mrs. Gracie Donovan.* She'd never imagined or expected that would be her name one day.

"Remember not to worry about anything. The kiddos and pets are all taken care of, so don't rush back from your honeymoon." Brianna hugged her again.

As everyone waved and saw them off, Gracie thought her heart might burst with joy. She'd never expected to fall in love with her neighbor and become a mother to precious twins, but the Lord had orchestrated the plans. And sometimes unexpected plans were the best of all.

THE END

After teaching the first grade and kindergarten for 21 years, Patti Jo had to retire early due to severe spinal/back problems. She saw this as an opportunity to fulfill her dream of writing full-time, which she loves. A life-long Georgia girl, Patti Jo loves Jesus, her family, and cats. She's blessed to be a Forget-Me-Not Author, and when not writing she loves spending time with family---especially her precious grandbaby. Patti Jo loves connecting with readers, and you can find her on Facebook at Author Patti Jo Moore, or visit her blog at https://catmomscorner.blogspot.com

AN UNEXPECTED ROMANCE is the second book in her Emerald Coast Romances series.
The first book is A SEASIDE ROMANCE.

Enjoy the first chapter below:

1

Emma Jean Hopkins gazed out the window of her bungalow, enjoying a dolphin close to the shore. Past the beach of sugary sand, she watched the creature leap playfully in the teal water, the sun shimmering on its slick skin. *Not a care in the world.* Would she ever feel that way again?

After all, wasn't the reason she moved to Coastal Breeze, Florida, to forget about her past and move forward, without having to look over her shoulder all the time? Her ringing cell phone snapped her from her thoughts.

A smile spread across her face as Jeb Hopkins' southern drawl came through the phone. "How's my favorite daughter doing today?" He chuckled in his customary good-natured way, and Emma could visualize her overall-clad father standing by the kitchen window of the cozy farm home, sipping his morning coffee.

She giggled. "Hi, Dad. Your favorite—and only— daughter is doing fine, thanks. How are you? I hope the farm isn't making you work too hard." Concern laced her voice for her sixty-two-year old father exerting himself on the twenty-acre family farm in South Georgia.

"Nah, don't worry none about me. Working hard is what keeps me going, you know. Besides, these farmhands I got are a big help." He cackled, and Emma could envision his tanned face and whiskered chin.

Without warning a twinge of something— homesickness?—tugged at her heart, and she drew in a deep breath. If her father thought for one second she was homesick, he'd hop in his pick-up truck and drive to the Florida panhandle as fast as he could.

Besides, he had been through enough in the past two years with problems on the farm and the loss of Emma's mother, so he wouldn't want his baby girl to be unhappy.

She continued talking so he wouldn't suspect a hint of melancholy had crept in. "I think that once I adjust to my new town and get into a routine of running the gift shop, everything will be great. I can't wait for you to come and visit." She prepared herself for her father's usual response whenever he was invited anywhere.

"I'd love to see you, Em. But you know how busy this farm keeps me. And I sure don't have the energy I used to, especially with my ol' arthritis acting up now and then. I promise you I'll get down there one of these days, and you know you can call me anytime if you need anything."

"I know, Dad. Thanks. And don't worry—Aunt Ginny has been wonderful." Fighting the lump in her throat, she changed the subject by inquiring about her favorite goat and the other farm animals. Ten minutes later their call ended.

Okay, time to get going. She finished the last few swigs of her coffee and got dressed. Tomorrow the gift shop would be reopening, but today she'd dress in jeans and a tee shirt, with minimum makeup. No sense in wearing better clothes if she was going to be by herself most of the day arranging items on shelves, checking inventory lists, and general cleaning duties.

Heading out of the cottage, Emma breathed in the warm April air blowing in from the gulf. She pulled her chestnut hair into a ponytail and lifted her face to the sunshine. Sometimes she still couldn't believe she lived at the Florida coast. The view of the ocean from her windows often made her feel she was dreaming, especially when the dolphins were frolicking along the emerald coast.

Before climbing into her car for the short drive to her aunt's shop, Emma noticed the brilliant blue sky. Puffs of clouds floated toward the west, reminding her of cotton balls her mother had always kept in a small jar in their home.

Mother. How she missed her sweet mom, though Emma would not have wanted the poor woman to linger in pain any longer. The horrible cancer had ravaged Shirley Hopkins' body and her passing had been a blessing in that respect. Yet grief had overwhelmed Emma and her family at the time, and two years hadn't lessened her sense of loss.

After parking in the small lot adjacent to the store, Emma hurried to the glass door and knocked. She grinned as she saw her aunt hurrying to let her in.

"Good morning, my sweet niece." Aunt Ginny planted a quick kiss on Emma's cheek, then drew back and looked at her. "Even dressed casually for work, you're still a beauty, Emma Jean. It amazes me that you're not married with a couple of little ones around you." The middle-aged woman clicked her tongue before continuing. "But when the right man does come along, you'll be ready. I still hate what you went through with that no-good thug, may he rest in peace." Ginny shook her head, then grabbed Emma's hand and pulled her to the counter.

"I'm just happy you've offered me this opportunity to live and work in Coastal Breeze, Aunt Ginny. It's so different from being on the farm, but I already like it a lot."

"Well, I'm sure the scenery is different, but I guess the heat and humidity are what you're used to." Her aunt smiled.

"Oh yes, good ol' South Georgia summers are plenty hot and humid, but at least here there's a nice breeze from the ocean." She released a sigh and smiled. "I really do think I'll be happy here." Eager to get to work, Emma was certain her social-butterfly aunt had things to do.

"I sure hope and pray you are, sweetheart. Now, you've got my cell number if you need me today. I'm meeting my stitchery group for lunch over in Destin, and then plan to run a few errands. But I can scoot back here in a flash if you need me. Remember to keep the door locked and I've got snacks and soft drinks in the supply room, so help yourself."

After a few general instructions about a small amount of inventory to be listed and shelved, Ginny was out the door, her citrusy cologne scenting the air behind her.

To Emma's relief the time passed quickly, and she didn't have any problems with the jobs she needed to accomplish. Who knows? Maybe running a small gift shop would be a good fit for her and she'd enjoy it much more than she'd expected. It would certainly be different than working in the daycare center back in her hometown.

About one o'clock, her stomach rumbled, and she decided she needed more than snack crackers and a bottled water. After locking the gift shop, she drove to a nearby fast-food restaurant and picked up her lunch.

The cheeseburger, fries, and cola weren't the healthiest choice for a midday meal, but today it would do and it gave her a boost of energy. About an hour after eating, Emma was rearranging some figurines on a shelf when a knock sounded at the door.

The noise startled her so much she almost dropped a small mouse figurine. Her heart pounded as she tried to decide whether to answer the door or duck down and hide behind a shelf. *Oh, good grief, don't be ridiculous. The person has most likely seen you already, and maybe whoever it is only needs directions.* Not that she'd be much help in that area.

Slowly making her way toward the glass door, Emma was surprised to see a well-dressed man who appeared to be close to her age. With neatly trimmed brown hair and dark eyes, he was tall, and his business suit seemed to emphasize his broad shoulders. Was Aunt Ginny expecting a sales representative today? No, her organized aunt would've mentioned that, and she would not have left Emma on her own.

With shaking hands, she inched the door open and gazed up at the stranger. "Yes?" To her dismay the one word came out as a timid squeak, much like the mouse figurine she'd almost dropped might make had it been a real mouse.

The man smiled with a curious tilt of his head. "I'm sorry, is this store not open?"

Aaaugh…she'd forgotten to hang the CLOSED sign on the door. Emma reached up and tucked some wayward strands of hair behind her ear as she attempted to maintain a calm and confident manner, even though she was nowhere close to feeling that way at the moment.

"No, I'm sorry but the gift shop is closed until tomorrow. We'll be opening at ten o'clock in the morning." For some strange reason she had the sudden urge to invite the stranger inside the store and offer him one of the colas that Aunt Ginny kept in the supply room. No! She didn't know this man and absolutely could not permit him to step inside the shop.

She was relieved when he nodded and gave her a wide grin—one that only made his handsome face even more handsome.

"Okay, no problem. Sorry I disturbed you."

"Oh, you didn't disturb me. I was just doing some work since the shop reopens tomorrow. I'd forgotten to hang the CLOSED sign on the door, and I'm really sorry we're not open yet." What was wrong with her? She was rambling like a lonely person starved for attention.

"Well, since you'll be open tomorrow, I'll try to stop by on my way back home to Alabama." He hesitated as if wanting to say more, but didn't. "Thank you again." With a pleasant nod, the good-looking stranger turned and headed toward his sleek sports car parked in the adjacent lot.

She stood at the door and stared as he walked away, and for a reason she couldn't explain, she had a letdown feeling as he climbed into his car. *Get a grip, Emma.* For all she knew this man could be some kind of con artist or have a sketchy background. It was probably a blessing he didn't linger any longer.

Yet returning to her task of arranging figurines, she found herself hoping he'd stop by the next day. Even if he didn't purchase anything, she wanted to see him again.

~ ~ ~

Why had he knocked on the gift shop door? It should've been obvious that the store wasn't open for business. Yet he'd been eager to purchase a birthday gift for his sister and he knew Avril would appreciate something from the Florida coast.

On second thought, maybe it had been a blessing he'd knocked at the door because the pretty worker who answered was a sight for his tired, overworked eyes. As if to emphasize how hard he had been working lately, his cell phone rang at that moment.

"Thomas Wilton here." He hoped his voice didn't carry the exhaustion he felt.

"Hello Thomas. It's Mac Chandler, in the main office. Am I catching you at a bad time?"

Thomas's pulse quickened, and his hand gripped the steering wheel tightly. Maybe he should pull off the road into a parking lot somewhere so he could focus on this conversation. It wasn't everyday he received a phone call from the company's co-founder.

"Hello, Mr. Chandler. No, this is fine. I'm just driving back to my hotel in Destin at the moment, so I can talk." Yeah, he definitely needed to pull off the road. Thankfully a fast-food restaurant was up ahead so he was able to whip into the small parking lot.

Breathing a sigh of relief, he could now focus on the call. He grabbed his satchel in the passenger seat with his free hand and took out a small notebook and a pen. It might not be a bad idea to jot notes as Mr. Chandler talked—especially given how tired he was at the moment.

"Well, I'm glad I caught you, because we've

recently had a board meeting and you've been recommended to take over the Florida territory for Coastal Industries. I'd much prefer giving you this information in person, but I wanted to go ahead and let you know so you could give it some thought. Now, don't feel pressured about letting us know. Take some time to pray over this major decision and career move. You can take up to two weeks if needed, because the position will involve continued traveling and handling a bit more work. But we're always here to support you, so don't ever feel you're in this alone. You can call on myself or Ben Groves at any time with questions or if you need additional help. I do hope you'll consider this offer and give it serious thought. And by the way, it also includes a ten-percent pay increase, so that's something else to consider. Since you're a single man, you might not have a lot of expenses at the moment. However, once you settle down and have a family, this added income would be mighty handy." Mr. Chandler chuckled, his southern accent prominent in his comments.

Thomas knew it was a blessing he'd pulled off the main road and into a parking lot, otherwise he might've swerved onto the curb as he heard his boss's reason for calling.

A few seconds of silence hung in the air before Thomas cleared his throat and attempted to sound professional. "Thank you, Mr. Chandler. This is certainly an unexpected offer, and I'm deeply humbled and grateful. I will give this serious thought and let you know within the two-week time frame. You have my word." *Good grief, I sound like I'm negotiating a deal between two countries.* Yet at that moment he felt more honored and esteemed than he ever had, so for him this was a huge deal.

After a few more general comments about the weather and the current baseball season, the call ended.

Thomas sat for a few minutes, absorbing the news he'd just received. He wasn't sure if he felt like giving a whoop of joy or shuddering at the giant workload he knew would be placed upon his shoulders should he accept this position. But one thing was certain, and that was how fortunate he was to work at a Christian-based company who valued their employees. Yes, he had a lot of praying to do.

The next morning Thomas hurried to his car, clutching a cup of hotel coffee. He'd already checked out and his one bag was in his trunk. Now he'd head to his appointment with a hotel manager in Miramar, and then he was free to drive back home to Alabama. Except for one stop in Coastal Breeze. Yes, he'd swing by the little gift shop and purchase something for his sister. At the thought of seeing the pretty woman he'd spoken with the day before, his heart rate quickened. What was wrong with him? He knew absolutely nothing about her except for the fact she worked in a gift shop in a tiny coastal community.

Focus on this meeting. He chided himself while pulling into the large hotel parking lot. Palm trees swayed in the warm morning breeze and a few hotel guests walked to and from their cars. It was only April, yet most of the hotels were already doing a heavy business. In the peak tourist season of summer, it would be packed, he knew.

Entering the well-furnished lobby, Thomas was thankful he'd worn a nice suit. This hotel was upscale compared to many of their other clients. A clerk behind the guest counter smiled, eyeing him with appreciation. Her blond hair and tanned skin seemed to echo the fact she worked at a coastal hotel and was no doubt in the sun a lot. With brightly-painted nails and matching lipstick, she would be considered attractive to many men, yet Thomas tended to shy away from that look. The image of his previous girlfriend flashed in his mind. He shoved away the bitter memories of his last relationship.

"May I help you?" The clerk leaned toward the counter and her strong perfume reached Thomas's nose, making it itch.

"Good morning. I have a ten o'clock appointment with Mr. Wallace."

The woman's eyes lingered on his face a moment, making him feel awkward. He was more than ready to have this meeting and move on with his day.

The clerk looked down at a ledger on the counter and nodded. "Yes, Mr. Wallace should be in the main meeting room. I'm sure it's been reserved for the two of you to meet privately. I'll take you to him." She stepped out from behind the counter and wiggled a finger at him, indicating he was to follow.

He was thankful Ms. Clerk with the heavy make-up and perfume wouldn't be in their meeting. Not usually one to judge, Thomas couldn't help being a little wary of this woman.

She walked slowly in her stiletto heels down a carpeted hallway, then stopped at a closed door. Tapping lightly, she leaned toward the door and called out Mr. Wallace's name.

Then she quickly turned back to Thomas and winked. "He's all yours. Have a nice meeting." She stiletto-walked her way back down the hall toward the lobby, leaving the heavy perfume scent trailing behind.

Just as Thomas stepped into the meeting room, he sneezed. *Great. What a way to enter a meeting with a client.* Reaching into his pocket, he lifted out a linen handkerchief—silently thanking his grandmother for the gift many Christmases ago—and tried to discreetly wipe his nose.

Mr. Wallace stood from the table and smiled, extending a hand. "Good morning, Thomas. I hope my directions were helpful and you didn't get lost in the maze of hotels." The large man laughed good-naturedly, putting Thomas at ease.

"No sir, your directions were perfect. Thank you for meeting with me today, Mr. Wallace."

"Please, call me Chip. No formalities here." With a shake of his head and a slight grin, he continued. "I see you've met Devonna, one of our clerks." He blew out a sigh that could be interpreted as frustration. "Please don't misunderstand me, since we've only just met. But she's the hotel owner's daughter and that is why she works at the main desk. That's all I'll say for now." The look he gave Thomas backed up his own first impressions of the woman. It would appear that Chip Wallace wasn't thrilled with the image Devonna presented to those entering the hotel.

"Would you like some coffee? Or cola or water? The temperature is already climbing today, I can feel it."

Thomas politely declined, then opened his business satchel and took out his notebook. He was pleased with Chip Wallace's reaction to the suggestions he outlined for the hotel.

To his delight, Thomas was out of the meeting in under two hours. And there was no further communication with the clerk. He strode briskly toward his car enjoying the bright sunshine streaming down on him and hearing the distant squawk of gulls, searching for their lunch at the nearby beach. He inhaled a deep breath of ocean air, feeling positive that this would be a good day. After all, with the exception of the staring clerk, everything else had gone great. Now to head to Coastal Breeze, then home to Alabama.

Driving along the main highway that led into Coastal Breeze, he pondered gift ideas for Avril. What would give his handicapped sister a big smile? She liked so many things, but he wanted to give her something really special.

About ten minutes later he pulled into the parking lot for *Ginny's Treasures by the Sea,* and noticed a few other cars in the lot, which was a good sign. Thomas always felt sorry for small, independent businesses that couldn't compete with large chain stores.

As he opened the door, a small bell tinkled overhead, and a delightful scent of something fresh and citrusy greeted him. Would he see the pretty employee he'd spoken with the previous day? Instead, an older woman greeted him and he felt a stab of disappointment.

"Welcome to Ginny's. May I help you find something today?" She wore a turquoise dress with bright jewelry and her voice was warm. Despite the fact she must be in her sixties, she exuded energy and had a youthful sparkle in her eyes.

"Thank you. I'm looking for a gift for a twenty-three-year-old woman. I guess I'll just look around, if that's okay."

"Oh certainly, honey. You take your time, but if you need help let me know. And by the way, my name is Ginny so feel free to holler if you need assistance." She gave him another warm smile before turning to help two women who were asking her opinion about a small lamp.

He thanked her and gathered his wits to see what was available in the shop. Specifically, he needed something that Avril would really like.

Scented candles were displayed in an attractive setting, with tiny seashells sprinkled among them. As Thomas moved on, he saw figurines—most with a nautical theme—and other small decorative items for someone's home—gift baskets, scented lotions, jewelry, small ocean-themed framed prints, and even greeting cards. He decided Ginny had an eclectic kind of gift shop, carrying an assortment of items. Now, what to buy for his sister?

A female voice spoke and he jerked his head to the right. The woman from the day before! Except today she looked even prettier.

She smiled at him. "Did you need some help?"

He tried not to stare. Was she the same woman? Yes, it had to be. Yet today she was dressed in nicer clothes—not fancy, but a coral-colored Capri outfit with a small sailboat stitched on the front. Her shoulder-length chestnut hair hung loosely, framing a pretty face with green eyes and a mouth that looked as if it smiled easily. For some reason the word *wholesome* came to mind. A far cry from the hotel clerk he'd encountered earlier that day. Or his ex-girlfriend, Courtney.

Thomas shrugged. "Thanks, I'm just looking around. I need a gift for a twenty-three-year-old woman, so I'm sure I'll find something here she'll like."

"Okay, I'm Emma if you need any help. And my Aunt Ginny is here too if you have questions. I'm new and still learning, but I'm happy to help any way I can." She offered another smile, then turned and headed to a customer trying to decide on some earrings.

Thomas remained where he was, watching Emma walk away. He'd glanced at her hands and hadn't noticed a ring, but that didn't always mean anything. Why did he feel so drawn to her?

Snapping himself out of his thoughts about the beautiful employee, he stepped over to the scented lotions and sniffed a couple of bottles. Yes, Avril would like these. One was honeysuckle and the other jasmine. Not too heavy, but nice feminine scents.

Clutching the two bottles of lotion, he was about to head to the counter to pay but stopped. His attention was captured by a small lighthouse figurine, and he knew Avril would love it. Carefully lifting it from the display, he then stepped to the checkout counter to pay.

No one was behind the counter, so he stood there

with the items placed near the register.

"Are you ready?" Emma hurried toward him.

"Yes, these should be perfect." He grinned and took out his wallet.

Emma rang up the lotions and the lighthouse, then wrapped everything before placing the items in a bag. As she reached her hand out to accept his payment, their hands touched.

Her skin was so smooth. Did she notice their contact? The quick glance she gave him answered his silent question.

A shy, hesitant smile slightly curved Emma's lips, and she ducked her head as she placed the money into the cash register drawer. "Thank you for shopping at Ginny's. If you're in the area again, please feel free to stop by."

Was she giving him a standard line she was trained to use on customers, or could she possibly want him to stop by again?

He gave a smiling nod. "Thank you, Emma. I'll definitely be in the area again since I travel for my job, so I'm sure I'll stop here in the future. Your aunt has a very nice shop."

She reached up and tucked a strand of hair behind one ear, revealing a small sailboat earring. "Yes, Aunt Ginny has worked hard and is very proud of her little shop. I've recently moved here to help her run it."

"Oh? Where are you from?"

"South Georgia. I grew up on a farm in the tiny town of Westville. You've probably never heard of it." She giggled, a blush tinting her pretty face.

Thomas feigned a frown and laughed. "No, sorry I haven't. I'm from the Montgomery area of Alabama, but travel in Florida for my job. I'm with Coastal Industries, and you've probably never heard of that company." He laughed again, pleased to see her grinning as she shook her head. Then he added. "My name is Thomas, by the way. Thomas Wilton."

She grinned, but then someone else caught her attention, and Thomas

realized two women were standing behind him waiting to pay for their purchases. He needed to leave but didn't want to. As he said good-bye, he promised to stop in her aunt's shop again.

Driving back to Alabama, Thomas couldn't stop thinking about the attractive employee. She was a farm girl from South Georgia now working in a small gift shop on the Florida coast. What a different life this must be for her.

As he continued the three-hour drive, various thoughts whirled through his mind. The phone call from Mr. Chandler offering the promotion, his meeting with the hotel manager that morning, and meeting an attractive lady named Emma who worked in a gift shop. Yet the one thought that dominated and pleased him the most was thinking of Emma, and Thomas knew without a doubt he would be stopping by that shop again. The sooner the better.

~ ~ ~

Why had she babbled on so much to that customer? Sure, he was attractive and tall and wore a nice business suit. Not to mention his sleek little sports car. But for all Emma knew he might be married. Yeah, she'd heard stories of businessmen who traveled and met women in different cities and deceived them. No, she absolutely would not let herself be deceived again—ever. After what she'd experienced with BG she could never go through that again.

"Emma, you've worked so hard today, honey. It's almost two o'clock and you need to eat your lunch. Go on to the supply room and take a break. I can handle the shop, and I've already munched some snacks between my customers, so I'm not hungry." Ginny patted her shoulder and Emma knew it would do no good to argue with her aunt.

"Okay, I'll eat the sandwich I brought, but if it gets busy out here, you holler. I won't be long." She wasn't about to tell her aunt she doubted if she could even get down the peanut butter sandwich she'd brought. After her brief chat with Thomas, her stomach had been doing cartwheels.

Yet as she nibbled at her sandwich and small bag of chips, she remembered that Thomas   had mentioned he was purchasing a gift for a twenty-three-year-old woman. Hmm…possibly his girlfriend? What did it matter? She might never see him again.

She didn't have time to mull over that last thought because the chattering she heard from the shop indicated business had picked up. Her aunt would need her help, so Emma took another sip of cola and hurried out to assist.

Ginny looked at her in amazement. Sure enough, there were now close to twenty customers milling around the shop. Hopefully these people weren't only browsing because more sales would help prepare for the upcoming summer season.

Pasting on a smile, Emma stepped over to an older lady who was admiring the jewelry selection. "Did you need any help?"

"No thank you, dear. I'm just looking, but I have a feeling I'll be purchasing one of these bracelets. They are so cute with the little nautical charms on them."

"Yes, ma'am, they are. I confess those are one of my favorite items in Aunt Ginny's shop." She grinned at the elderly lady, who had on bright pink lipstick that matched a pink ensemble she wore, including dangling pink flamingo earrings.

The woman paused and eyed Emma. "Is Ginny your

aunt? Is that what you said, dear? My hearing isn't so keen anymore." She chuckled and shook her head, the curls in her silver hair bouncing along with her earrings.

"Yes, ma'am. I'm Ginny's niece, Emma Hopkins. I've recently moved here from South Georgia to help out in the gift shop."

"That is wonderful! So nice to meet you, Emma. My name is Mildred Weatherbee, but my friends call me Midge. I know Ginny from church, and of course, the times when I've shopped here." She continued smiling at Emma, then reached out and lifted a bracelet from the small stand. "I think I will go ahead and buy this, and I'll be stopping in again soon. I need to get on to the grocery store before my legs give out. Ah, the joys of getting old." She chuckled and shook her head.

After ringing up the sale, Emma smiled at her. "It was nice to meet you, Mrs. Weatherbee." She handed the small bag across the counter.

The woman laughed and playfully shook a finger at her. "I insist you call me Midge. Besides, it'll make me feel younger." She laughed again as Emma agreed to use her nickname.

After the woman exited the shop, Ginny hurried over to Emma. "Oh, I didn't get to speak to Midge. She's a sweetheart, although some folks think she's a bit of a busybody. But she means well." Ginny straightened a few knick-knacks at the counter, then peered directly at her niece. "How are things going for you? Not too overwhelming, I hope. Please don't tell me you're ready to return to the farm." She winked and reached out to pat Emma's hand.

"No worries. It's going well, and I guess I shouldn't spend so much time on one customer, but that lady was very kind." Emma was relieved when her aunt assured her she was going a great job.

"Besides, if my customers don't feel they're getting

a warm welcome and friendly service, they can easily shop elsewhere." She grinned before hurrying off to assist several women in the home décor section.

The remainder of the day passed quickly, even though business tapered off closer to suppertime. Emma was surprised at how tired she was and looked forward to the soft bed in her cottage.

"Are you sure you don't want to come to my house for supper? I've got a leftover casserole to reheat and it would be plenty to share." Ginny eyed her with a bit of concern.

"That's so sweet, but I'll be fine. I stocked my refrigerator and pantry with enough food to hold me awhile, and I'll heat up some soup and do some reading tonight. Thank you anyway." It gave Emma a sense of security knowing she wasn't all alone in her new town. Not that she had anyone to fear in Coastal Breeze—the dangers had been left behind in South Georgia.

A few minutes later she unlocked her cottage door, glad to be home. As she enjoyed her soup and relaxed that evening, her mind returned to her day at the gift shop. At least being so busy had prevented her from dwelling on the handsome customer earlier in the day. But she couldn't deny that she hoped he'd stop in her aunt's store again. Very soon.

AN UNEXPECTED ROMANCE